I0724677

FALLEN MESSENGERS BOOK TWO

SPELLBOUND

AVA MARIE SALINGER

COPYRIGHT

Spellbound (Fallen Messengers #2)
Copyright © 2021 by Ava Marie Salinger.
All rights reserved.
Registered with the US Copyright Office.
Third paperback edition: 2024
ISBN:978-1-912834-22-8

www.AMSalinger.com
shop.adstarrling.com

Edited by Right Ink On The Wall

❧

The right of Ava Marie Salinger to be identified as the author of this work has been asserted in accordance with the Copyright, Designs and Patents Act 1988. No part of this book may be reproduced in any form or by any electronic or mechanical means, including information storage and retrieval systems, without written permission from the author, except for the use of brief quotations in a book review. Your respect of the author's rights and hard work is appreciated. This book is a work of fiction. References to real people (living or dead), events, establishments, organizations, or locations are intended only to provide a sense of authenticity, and are used factitiously. All other characters, and all other incidents and dialogue, are drawn from the author's imagination and are not to be construed as real.

FALLEN MESSENGERS GLOSSARY

Aerial: An angel or demon who can control wind.

Alchemist: A human who can create new matter or manipulate existing matter into new forms. Emits a scent of powdered iron.

Aqueous: An angel or demon who can control water.

Argent Lake: Home of the Naiads.

Argonaut Agency: Organization responsible for law and order in the supernatural and magical communities. Headquarters in New York. Agents include angels, demons, and magic users.

Astrea Sea: Home of the Nereids.

Bloodsand: A black tree with red veins that grows in

the Nine Hells. Created by warlocks who made pacts with the Underworld after the Fall. Can be used to summon war demons from the Nine Hells.

Blossom Silver: A silver derivative that can heal injuries caused by demonic weapons or black magic. Made by the Naiads.

Cabalista: Demonic organization. Agents include demons only. Headquarters in London.

Dark Blight: A powder black-magic users use in their rituals and which is poisonous to angels and other magic users. Made by Shadow Empire alchemists from the heart of a Dryad.

Demi: The offspring of a God of Heaven/God of the Underworld and a human or a being possessing divine powers. Can take on any appearance.

Electrum: Naturally occurring alloy of gold and silver, as well as copper and other trace elements. Used extensively by Argonaut in their weapons. Combined with steel, titanium, and Rain Silver to make their bullets.

Empyreal: The highest order of angels or demons, with powers equal to those of a Demigod.

Enchanter/Enchantress: A human who uses illusion magic. Emits a scent of cedar.

Fiery: An angel or a demon who can wield Heaven or Hell's Fire.

Fractured Soul: A human's damaged soul core, extracted from the body – a powerful source of magic.

Ghoul: An evil spirit who consumes the flesh of humans. Emits a scent of rotting meat.

Glitterfang: A pale powder white-magic users employ in their rituals and which is poisonous to demons and black-magic users. Made by Nereids.

Hexa: Guild of magic users. Agents include magic users only. Headquarters in Seattle.

Incubus: A male demon who gains power from sleeping with humans and divine entities.

Ivory Peaks: Home of the Dryads.

Lucifugous: A heliophobic demon who abhors light and who can control darkness.

Mage: A human who uses an arcane staff to focus their magic powers. Emits a scent of Juniper.

Magic Levels: Classification of magic users based on their abilities, with Level Six being the weakest and Level One the strongest.

Messengers: Those belonging to the Third Sphere of Heaven and Third Hierarchy of Demons.

Order of Rosen: Religious order affiliated with the Catholic Church. Agents include angels only. Headquarters in Rome.

Rain Silver: A liquid-silver derivative that can injure and kill demons. Made by the Nymphs.

Rain Vale: Home of the Nymphs.

Reaper: A soul collector and guide of the dead. Emits a scent of camphor.

Reaper Seed: A drug that can intoxicate most beings and which is fatal in high doses. Mined by Lucifugous demons in the Shadow Empire. Potent hallucinogen for Lucifugous demons.

Shadow Empire: Home of Ghouls, Lucifugous demons, and Dark Alchemists.

Sorcerer/Sorceress: A human born with powerful soul core magic. Uses the energies around them to manipulate magic. Emits the scent of Valerian.

Soul Core: A living being's life force. Red for demons, white for angels, and dirty gray for humans.

Spirit Realm: Home of Pan, the Gods of the Underworld, and lesser spirits.

Stark Steel: Strongest and most magic-resistant metal on Earth. Found exclusively in the weapons and armor of the Fallen.

Succubus: A female demon who gains power from sleeping with humans and divine entities.

Terrene: An angel or demon who can control earth and its derivative metals.

The Fall: An unexplained event five hundred years ago that resulted in an army of angels and demons falling to Earth.

The Fallen: Angels or demons who fell to Earth.

The Nether: The space between Heaven, Earth, and the Nine Hells.

The Abyss: A forgotten realm beyond the Nether from where there is no escape.

War Demon: Demon soldiers created for battle. Remnants of an ancient war between Heaven and Hell. Banished to the deepest parts of the Hells.

Warlock: A human who draws power from demons

and the Hells and converts it to magic. Emits a scent of sulfur.

Wizard/Witch: A human who learns to use magic through spell books, and who utilizes potions and rituals to access their soul-core magic. Emits a scent of Frankincense.

CHAPTER ONE

Eden Monroe couldn't shake the feeling that she was being followed.

She gripped the straps of her backpack, ducked into a side alley, and emerged onto Vallejo Street. Still, the eerie feeling persisted. She glanced uneasily over her shoulder.

There was no one behind her.

Eden frowned.

I lost the Hexa guards at Lafayette Park. Who the hell could be trailing me now?

Having been the subject of the magic bureau's monitoring for as long as she could remember, Eden didn't doubt her instincts. She quickened her steps, hoping to lose whoever was tracking her. She really needed some comfort food today and her favorite burger place was only two streets over.

A peal of laughter made her tense. Eden stopped, her head snapping around.

A group of girls was walking along the opposite

pavement, their faces bright in the sunlight as they chatted animatedly. Her racing pulse slowed when she saw their uniforms.

They weren't from Saint Helena High.

Irritation surged through her as she slowly resumed walking. She'd promised herself she would stop caring about what happened at school. A grimace twisted her mouth. That was hard to do when her classmates seemed intent on provoking her, like they had done today.

As the only child of the director of the San Francisco Hexa bureau, Eden was the focus of constant attention. But it wasn't praise and admiration that were lavished on her on a daily basis by her peers. It was contempt and scorn.

Eden was the only student at Saint Helena High who couldn't use magic. In fact, she was the only child of a powerful magic user born without magic in her soul core. Despite begging her mother for months to send her to an ordinary human school, Brianna Monroe had insisted on enrolling her at the main academy for magic users in San Francisco, where she would attend magic theory classes even if she couldn't participate in the practical ones. Not only was Eden's mother a benefactor of the private school, but it was also where the children of all influential magic users in the city went to learn to control and develop their powers. Brianna's influence meant Eden had private tutors for normal, non-magic classes too.

She suspected her mother was aware of the abuse she suffered at the hands of her peers. Brianna had enough spies keeping an eye on her twenty-four-seven that she probably even knew her bathroom routine. As for the teachers at the academy, as long as no one harmed Eden physically, they would rather turn a blind eye to the bullying. She would only be at the school another two years and would never be anyone of importance in the magical community, so they saw no need to protect her or get in her good graces, despite running the risk of getting on her mother's bad side.

Eden spotted more students as she made her way to Union Street, their uniforms bright patches of color under the autumn sun. Located in the holy trifecta of Presidio Heights, Cow Hollow, and Pacific Heights, this area of San Francisco was home to most of the private schools in the city.

Eden shrugged past groups of girls and boys as she made her way to *Wild Burgers*, her shoulders hunched and her head down under the hood of her parka. Though she doubted any of them would recognize her, it didn't hurt to be safe. Relief darted through her when she entered the restaurant. It wasn't too crowded and there were plenty of empty seats left. She ordered a *Wild Spicy* chicken burger, fries, and a soda, and headed for the booth farthest back from the windows. It wouldn't take long for Hexa to find her and she intended to finish her meal well before then.

She'd just swallowed her last bite and was surreptitiously licking her fingers clean when the door opened and a guy walked in.

Eden stilled. So did most of the girls in the place.

The stranger's face was arresting, his chiseled

features perfectly formed, as if carved by the ancient Greek sculptors Eden liked to read about. His blue eyes were piercingly clear under his mop of honey-blond hair and he carried himself with a maturity that far exceeded his youthful appearance. He looked to be about eighteen and was currently wearing a heavy frown on said perfect face.

Eden swallowed.

The stranger's gaze swiveled and locked on her. Her stomach flip-flopped. Then he was moving, his long strides taking him to the counter, his head turning away dismissively.

Eden didn't realize she was holding her breath until he left a moment later, two large paper bags in hand. She could tell by the disappointed expressions of the girls in the restaurant that they wished he'd taken a table to eat there. She exhaled raggedly, puzzled by the strange feeling that had come over her when he'd looked at her.

She felt hot and cold, as if she were running a fever.

Eden went to the washroom and startled at the sight of her flushed cheeks in the mirror above the sink. She slapped cold water onto her face and told herself she was being an idiot. Sure, the guy had been hot, but she wasn't the kind of girl who got dazzled by just good looks. She averted her gaze from her reflection as she dried her hands, hating the blue eyes and blonde hair which resembled her mother's so much. She headed out onto Union Street and turned west, still mystified by her reaction to the stranger.

On a positive note, at least it took my mind off what happened today, if only for a moment.

Her belly clenched as she recalled the sneering faces of the girls who'd picked on her that afternoon. They'd stood around her and laughed as she took her drenched gym wear out of her locker. The gym teacher hadn't even blinked when Eden had excused herself from class, only murmuring under her breath that she would dock points from Eden's attendance records. Eden had just about managed to control her urge to throw her uniform at the woman's face, the rage burning through her so fierce she wanted to throw her head back and scream at the world.

But screaming and raging never got her anywhere.

Her mother was immune to her agony and her Hexa guards never bothered to deal with her tormentors.

Eden knew she was on her own. Had been on her own in that God-awful mansion since the moment she was born. She had no siblings or even cousins and had never known her father. Brianna never talked about him and there were no pictures of the couple anywhere in their home. The little Eden had gathered from overhearing gossiping Hexa attendants and housemaids was that he had been a magic user from Europe.

The only thing keeping her going was the knowledge that she would be free from her mother and Hexa in two short years. Free from the constant judgement of the woman who had given life to her and from those around her. Free from being found unworthy and inferior.

Once she officially became an adult, Eden intended to cut all ties with her mother and the magical community. She would disappear into this vast, wide world, to a place where no one knew who she was. Maybe then, she could start living instead of just surviving her current wretched existence.

She was approaching a music shop when the hairs rose on the back of her neck. Eden stiffened and slowed.

The eerie sensation of being tailed was back tenfold.

She stopped and gazed at the window to her left, her eyes not truly seeing the instruments on display. Instead, she focused on the reflection in the glass. She caught something shifting out of the corner of her eye.

Eden stared at the shadows under a tree fifty feet behind and to her right. Her pulse spiked.

There was something…odd about them. Something wrong.

Fear drenched Eden in a cold sweat. She turned and began walking briskly. Movement flickered at the edge of her vision. Eden whipped her head around and stared wide-eyed at the opposite pavement. Something was there. A hint of a shadow where none should have been.

A guttural rasp reached her from across the road. With it came the stench of rotting flesh. Eden gagged, covered her nose and mouth with a hand, and started running.

Startled cries and shouts followed her as she bumped into people, her heart beating so fast she thought she would faint. She'd just turned onto Steiner Street and was bolting up the hill when she heard footsteps behind her.

Panic squeezed her lungs, making it hard to breathe. Strands of blonde hair escaped the hood of her parka and danced around her face as she pumped her arms and legs, desperate to get away from her pursuers.

A garbled shout reached her. Eden ignored it and kept on running.

A hand grabbed her shoulder hard.

Eden whirled around, swung her bag at her attacker, and stumbled. The momentum of her awkward twist carried her to the ground. She gasped as she fell on her butt and grazed her palms.

"What the hell are you doing?!" Malik Garcia roared where he towered above her. "First you do your disappearing act, then you ignore our calls. Have you lost your mind, Eden?!"

Eden stared past the Hexa agent, blood thundering in her veins. "Did you see it? The shadow that was after me?!"

Malik scowled. "What shadow?"

He looked over his shoulder.

Eden blinked. The smell of rotting meat had disappeared. So had the sinister feeling that had heralded it.

Malik blew out a sigh as he looked down at her, two other Hexa guards closing in on them with frowns.

"Are you going to get up, or do you want me to carry you to the car?"

Eden bit back a sharp retort and slowly climbed to her feet.

The Hexa agents surrounded her as they headed for the Lincoln parked one street over, their ire palpable. Even though her home off Broadway wasn't far, there was no way they would let her walk. Not after her little stunt that afternoon.

Surprise danced through her when the car turned east. "Where are we going? I thought you were taking me to the house."

"Your mother wants to see you," Malik said curtly from the front passenger seat.

Eden's stomach dropped as they headed toward the financial district.

Now what?

CHAPTER TWO

"Hey, guys," Adrianne Hogan said testily through Cassius Black's earpiece. "You two know we're on a mission, right?"

Cassius Black tried to answer. Unfortunately, Morgan King's mouth was currently locked on his and stopping all attempts from him to communicate with their team. He pressed his hands subtly against Morgan's chest.

"I don't think they can hear you," Zach Mooney muttered to Adrianne across their comm line.

"Doesn't this count as harassment?" Bailey Green hazarded.

"You mean, is our esteemed leader physically molesting the newest member of our team?" Julia Chen drawled. "All evidence is currently pointing to that, yes."

The soft sigh that echoed through the earpiece could only have originated from Charlie Lloyd.

Morgan finally ended the kiss. The slow, sexy smile

the Aerial flashed at Cassius made his belly clench with desire.

He clamped down firmly on his burgeoning lust and narrowed his eyes at the angel smirking at him. "What are you doing?"

"Blending in," Morgan replied, unrepentant.

"I don't think it's working," Bailey said through their earpieces. "A group of witches practically fainted when they just walked past you."

"You guys stand out like sore thumbs," Adrianne muttered. "We should have had Zach and Julia on the ground instead of you two lovesick fools."

Cassius swallowed a sigh. Adrianne wasn't exactly wrong.

The hustle and bustle of the magic market under Chinatown rose around Cassius and Morgan where they stood under a bookshop awning. They were currently on the tail of an alchemist reputed to be selling second-rate Glitterfang to the community of magic users in San Francisco. The cocktail of rat poison and bleach-infused magic powder he'd been peddling had already landed scores of people in hospital. Though Hexa was gunning for the man's head, it was up to Argonaut as the agency responsible for law and order in the supernatural and magic communities to track down and arrest the criminal.

Their source had told them the alchemist would be making an appearance at the market today, although the wizard hadn't been certain of the exact location of the makeshift booth their target would erect.

Cassius, Morgan, and their team had been there for

two hours already and had yet to spot him. The physical description of the alchemist varied between his victims' accounts, making it clear he was using an illusion spell to mask his true identity. Cassius's ability to accurately detect the scent of a person's soul core meant they would be able to narrow down their options quickly once he made an appearance.

Cassius and Morgan joined the throng of people navigating the alleys, the glow of flame torches casting their shadows on the ground. Though it was still daytime, the underground market saw no natural light and was permanently bathed in a soft, orange twilight. Cassius knew the place would get even busier once the sun set. It was fortunate the alchemist hadn't chosen to come there at nighttime, when his scent would have been harder to filter out among the host of others that would have clouded the air.

A hint of something familiar drifted past Cassius's nostrils as they turned onto a narrow path in the eastern district a short while later. The San Francisco underground magic market was the biggest emporium of its kind on the west coast and spanned three city blocks. It was divided into five districts: north, south, east, west, and central. The central district was where the most expensive shops were located. It regularly attracted magic users from nearby cities, the variety of rare goods drawing them in despite the hefty price tags.

Cassius bumped into a witch, mumbled an apology, and carried on walking.

"You got something?" Morgan said lightly.

"Yes."

"Get ready to mobilize," Morgan warned the rest of their team.

Cassius tracked the scent of powdered iron and rat poison he'd just identified on the witch he'd brushed up against to a tent some two hundred feet from the closest exit. He eyed the gateway that led to Stockton Street for a moment, parted the flap of the tent, and entered the shadowy space beyond ahead of Morgan.

The scent of powdered iron grew stronger. It was characteristic of the soul core of an alchemist.

Though Cassius's preternatural eyes easily pierced the gloom, he squinted slightly, as if struggling to see for a moment. Rickety tables lined the floor around them. They were loaded with magical items, powders, and potions. Most of it looked legit.

A frail voice reached them from across the way. "Can I help you, gentlemen?"

Cassius's gaze swiveled to a plump, elderly woman in a black dress and hooded cape sitting on a padded chair behind the counter at the far end of the shop. She was knitting a scarf and had paused, her needles held aloft.

Cassius flashed her a smile. "We're just browsing."

"Then I shall leave you to it," the woman said magnanimously. "Do let me know if you need anything."

She picked up her knitting. Cassius and Morgan started perusing the goods.

"Oh." Cassius paused and turned, his face brightening as if recalling something. "I was actually thinking of getting some Glitterfang. Do you happen to have any?"

The clickety-clack of the knitting needles stilled. The woman looked up and studied them with a rheumy gaze that was sharper than it should have been.

"I do. I keep it in the back. Just give me a moment."

The woman rose and shuffled awkwardly through the beaded curtain behind her. For a second, Cassius feared she'd guessed their identities and was making a run for it. He focused on her soul core and was relieved to sense it was still close by.

She returned a moment later with a wooden chest. "This is a fresh batch I got yesterday." She opened the box. "Straight from the thighs of beautiful Nereids," she added with a cackle.

Cassius masked a grimace as he inspected the clear sachets of white powder packed neatly inside. Glitterfang was a key ingredient in white magic users' rituals. It was made by the sea spirits who lived on the Astrea Sea. Rumor had it that they crushed the flowers of the Glitterfang tree between their naked thighs to make the powder.

Rumor was wrong.

Cassius had been to the Astrea Sea on a few occasions in the past hundred years. The only things the goddesses of the sea crushed between their thighs were the heads of their enemies.

He lifted one of the sachets and sniffed it. "This is good."

The woman's grin widened.

"Let me guess. You used chamomile and sage to

mask the smell of rat poison and bleach?" Cassius added lightly.

The woman froze. Her expression turned ugly in the next instant. She twisted around and bolted through the beaded curtain, her movements no longer awkward.

Cassius and Morgan vaulted over the counter and went after her. Something exploded over them as they ran out of the rear of the tent.

"Shit!" Morgan cursed, wiping red powder from his face. "Did that bastard just use cayenne pepper on us?"

"Yeah."

The stinging in Cassius's nostrils and eyes faded as he drew on his seraphic powers to nullify the effect of the spice, his gaze locked on the fleeing figure's back. Just as he'd suspected, the alchemist was heading for the Stockton Street exit.

The man's body morphed back into its original form as he barged into the people in his path, his illusion spell scattering in his panic. Cassius and Morgan were a couple of steps behind him when he darted through the opening.

A pall of darkness descended upon them the moment they entered the passage.

CHAPTER THREE

"WHAT THE—?!" MORGAN EXCLAIMED.

Cassius frowned. He knew this power. *Lucifugous!*

He grabbed his dagger, unleashed his Stark Steel sword, and blocked the axe sailing toward his head. Wood smashed and splinters filled the air as the handle exploded. The axe blade sang past his face and thudded into the ground behind him.

"Are you okay?" Cassius asked Morgan, senses on high alert.

"Never better," the angel growled.

Wind swept over Cassius as Morgan let his Aerial powers loose. He released a pulse of his own Empyreal energy, the light emanating from his soul core wrapping around the turbulent currents and clearing the shadows around them in a flash.

Cassius studied the two dull-faced demons standing in their path. As heliophobes, the Lucifugous could control darkness and wield it as a weapon, blinding their victims' sight while they attacked.

"You guys should stop before things get ugly," he warned the pair.

The demons glanced at one another.

"*You* ugly," the one on the left said sullenly.

"He didn't hire the smartest cookies in the batch as his guards, huh?" Morgan muttered.

"How do you want to play this?"

Morgan sighed. "I'll handle Dumb and Dumber. You go after our guy."

The Lucifugous demons' eyes rounded as Cassius unfurled his wings.

"*Devil!*" the one on the right mumbled, staggering backward.

"Guardian of Light!" the second demon said hoarsely, his tone almost reverential.

Cassius leapt into the air. His black and red wings, so different from the gray ones of the other Fallen, had earned him worse names than devil. Guardian of Light was newer, however, and a title he'd only become aware of recently.

Steps appeared in the distance as he navigated the torch-lit tunnel, his feathers skimming the ceiling and walls. He accelerated and darted up them. A group of startled magic users came into view halfway up the stairs. Cassius rolled and flicked around them. Dazzling brightness framed the exit some hundred feet above him. He folded his wings as he emerged into the daylight and landed lightly on the pavement at the top.

A commotion to the left drew his gaze.

Julia was sitting on top of the alchemist on the dented roof of a Maserati parked at the curb.

"*Get off me, you bitch!*" the man yelled.

His face was puce and his chin peppered with spit where he struggled beneath her, hands and feet scrabbling uselessly at the metal as he attempted to shift the angel off him.

Julia didn't budge.

"Not until you say uncle." She paused. "And apologize for the bitch comment."

"How'd they get up there?" Cassius asked the rest of their team as they arrived at a light jog.

"She picked him up when he came out and dropped him on the car," Adrianne replied, her voice full of misplaced pride.

Cassius sighed at the Terrene angel. "You know the owner is gonna be pissed, right?"

Julia shrugged. "So?"

On cue, a loud wail rose behind them. "*My baby!*"

A man in a suit that probably cost Cassius's rent hurried past them and headed for the damaged vehicle, his fingers stretching his skin as he dragged his hands down his pale face.

He glared at the angel and the prisoner atop it. "What did you do to my car?!"

"I apologize, sir." Julia rose, snagged the alchemist by the back of his collar, and landed lightly on the curb. "Please rest assured that the Argonaut Agency will take care of the repairs to your vehicle."

Zach and Bailey cuffed the disgruntled alchemist and checked him over for hidden weapons and potions while Julia dealt with the Maserati owner.

"Take care of the repairs?!" The man scowled. "How is that going to help me in the meantime? I need my—"

He stopped talking. Julia had just smiled.

"Hmm." The guy blinked. "I mean—"

Julia indicated the coffee place on the corner of the block. "How about I take down your details over a drink?"

"Sure."

The man headed after Julia with a glazed expression.

Cassius made a face.

Like all the angels and demons who fell to Earth five hundred years ago, Julia was stunningly attractive. Humans couldn't resist the Fallen's looks at the best of times. They pretty much had zero chance when an angel or demon turned on the charm.

Adrianne watched the pair stroll away with an expression that was half awe, half disgust. "Wow."

"Where's Julia going?" Morgan said behind them.

Cassius turned. Relief danced through him.

The Aerial looked unharmed.

Though he'd known Morgan was more than strong enough to take on two Lucifugous demons on his own, Cassius had hated leaving him down there, in the dark.

"She's engaging in damage limitation," Adrianne said. "And a bit of PR."

Morgan frowned as Julia and the Maserati owner entered the coffee shop. "She knows she's still on duty, right?"

They stared at him.

"What?"

"That's the pot calling the kettle black, isn't it?" Adrianne said tartly. "You could barely keep your paws off Cassius all afternoon."

Cassius's ears grew warm. The sorceress wasn't wrong.

It had been a month since he'd officially become an Argonaut agent and joined Morgan's team. He and Morgan had grown even closer in that time, their relationship flourishing despite spending almost every waking hour together.

Not to mention every night.

Cassius swallowed a happy sigh.

He and Morgan had become even more intimate in the bedroom, their passion for one another unabated however many times they made love. The awakening of their powers following their clash with Chester Moran, the warlock who had wanted to tear the Nether open underneath San Francisco, meant their soul cores were now connected in ways neither angel had experienced before in their living memory. Ways that meant sex was breathtakingly, exquisitely pleasurable, to the point Cassius feared he would pass out from the intensity of the orgasms Morgan brought him to.

That they had known each other before the Fall was now also an irrefutable fact.

Morgan had dreamt of Cassius since he came to Earth, a confession that had rocked Cassius to the core when the Aerial had admitted to it shortly after they met. Cassius in turn had remembered Morgan's true name—Ivmir—the first time he had fought Chester

Moran. Though they could not recall much else about their lives before the Fall, Cassius was convinced they had been lovers.

Their suspicion regarding their likely status as Demigods was something neither angel had yet revealed to their team or Francis Strickland, the local Argonaut bureau director. That particular secret was one they wanted to hang on to for as long as they could.

No Demigods currently walked the Earth, most having chosen to dwell in the Spirit Realm or one of the other kingdoms torn from Heaven and the Hells. To have the world know that two such entities were freely navigating human society would pose challenges they would prefer to avoid.

"Call it in," Morgan told Adrianne as Zach and Bailey maneuvered the handcuffed alchemist into the back of an Argonaut van.

They headed back to the office. Julia turned up a short while later.

"How did it go with Maserati guy?" Adrianne said.

"He won't sue. And he's taking me out for dinner Saturday."

"What?" Adrianne gasped, horrified. "But—but—he's *old!*"

Cassius bit back a smile as half the agents in the bull pen stared at her in disbelief.

"Babe, she's like a gazillion times older than that guy," Bailey muttered.

Adrianne flashed a frown at the wizard at the endearment. They were former lovers. It was clear

Bailey wanted to remove the former from that equation. The sorceress, on the other hand, didn't appear to have forgiven him for whatever he'd done that had ended their relationship in the first place.

"That guy owns *Revelations*," Julia stated succinctly.

Adrianne sucked in air.

"Wait. You mean the new Michelin-starred restaurant that just opened up on North Beach?!" Bailey gasped.

"The very one."

"Ah." Zach smiled. "So, you're after the food, not the man."

Everyone in the bureau knew Julia would sell her soul to the devil for a gourmet meal.

"Exactly," the Terrene angel said, unabashed. "That dinner is gonna be worth at least three hundred dollars."

Morgan rolled his eyes hard.

CHAPTER FOUR

"Wʜᴀᴛ ᴅɪᴅ ʏᴏᴜ ᴊᴜsᴛ sᴀʏ?!" Eᴅᴇɴ ᴍᴜᴍʙʟᴇᴅ ʜᴏᴀʀsᴇʟʏ.

She stared at the woman behind the desk in front of her.

Brianna Monroe sat poised and cool, her perfectly manicured hands propped under her chin as she studied Eden impassively. Not a single strand of her blonde hair was out of place and no creases marred her custom-tailored, black pantsuit.

"You heard me correctly the first time. You will be enrolled in a magic college after you graduate from Saint Helena."

Brianna glanced to her left. Valerie Hartman, one of her aides, brought over a stack of brochures.

"You can pick any of those," the Hexa bureau director said with a perfunctory wave as Valerie handed Eden the pamphlets with a faintly apologetic smile. "I would have included the best magic colleges in Europe, too, were it not for your recent rebellious behavior."

Eden's heart slammed against her ribs. She gazed blindly at the pile of booklets in her hands. They felt heavy, like shackles that would drag her to the bottom of a fathomless sea. She swallowed.

The freedom she had yearned for was slipping away from her and there was apparently nothing she could do about it.

"Why?"

Brianna arched an eyebrow. "Why what?"

"Why are you doing this to me?"

Eden's vision blurred as she glared at her mother. She wiped her eyes with the back of a hand, angry at herself for crying. For a moment, she thought she saw a flash of pain and regret in Brianna's gaze. But Eden knew better.

The woman before her would never show her pity.

"I only want what's best for you," Brianna declared. "Your grades are good enough to land you a seat at any of those colleges. I don't see—"

"Grades?!" Anger swelled inside Eden. She flung the brochures on the desk, her self-restraint finally snapping. "What grades?! You don't have a clue what's going on with my school life, so how the hell would you know anything about my grades, mother?!"

Brianna frowned as the pamphlets scattered past her and fell to the floor. Valerie and one of the other aides went over to pick them up.

"Control your emotions, child."

Eden ignored the warning, too full of rage to care about decorum.

"Or what? What will you do?" she challenged.

Brianna pressed her hands down on the desk and rose to her feet, her beautiful face darkening.

"Do not provoke me, Eden," she snapped, her voice cold. "If you cannot act your age, then I will have you grounded."

"Oh, please," Eden scoffed. "I would relish that! At least I wouldn't have to see the hateful faces of my classmates and teachers!"

She masked her dismay behind a sneer. Being grounded meant she wouldn't be able to do the little things that brought her pleasure, like visiting her favorite burger place or going to the bookshops she loved to browse.

Brianna grew still. Her gaze swiveled to Malik. "I thought the bullying had stopped."

"I'm sorry," Malik murmured remorsefully. "I shall have a word with her teachers again."

Eden's breath choked in her throat at the despicable act being played out before her.

"Seriously?!" She gazed contemptuously at her guards and her mother's aides before focusing on Brianna. "You are all going to stand there and pretend like you actually care?! Like you aren't aware it has been happening for years?!"

"Stop it, Eden," Brianna warned. "You don't know what you're talking about."

Eden froze for a moment, a familiar agony stabbing through her at her mother's words. "Oh. Of course. Forgive me. I forget my position." She lifted her chin defiantly. "As the only non-magic-user in the room, I am evidently too much of a halfwit to grasp the simplest of matters."

Brianna stiffened.

A sick feeling twisted Eden's stomach. She knew she should stop talking. She could see she was only making the situation worse. But, like a dam that had burst its walls, the words wouldn't stop coming.

"I've always wondered what magic users see when they look at me. Am I even human in their eyes? Or am I just a fake? Someone who was unfortunate enough to be born in a position of privilege most magic users would kill for?" She clenched her fists, her nails digging into her palms. "Maybe that's why they treat me like the dirt beneath their feet. Like an animal that should be chained and dragged around the street. Like something that doesn't deserve to exist. Tell me." She twisted on her heels, her hot gaze sweeping the shocked faces around her. "What *do* you see when you look at me? Do you see a girl? Or do you see a magicless puppet sitting on a throne? A useless, contemptible, pitiable bag of flesh and bones chained to her queen's will? *TELL ME!*"

Her roar drew gasps from her guards and Brianna's aides.

"Eden," Valerie mumbled, fingers over her mouth and face ashen.

"Don't do this," Brianna said bitterly. "You'll only hurt yourself."

Her mother had crossed the room, fingers raised as if to touch her arm. Eden hadn't heard her move. Brianna faltered before dropping her hand at her side, a frustrated expression flitting across her face. As she stared into the blue eyes opposite her, Eden knew she was effectively burning her bridges right now. But this latest act by Brianna was one she could not endure. Not when it meant more years of suffering ahead.

"Since when did you give a damn about whether I get hurt or not?"

Brianna recoiled as if she had been slapped.

"When will you be brave enough to admit that I am but a thorn in your side, mother?" Eden continued in the same lifeless voice. She pressed a hand to her chest. "Had I been born with magic, I'm sure you would have loved and cherished me."

The flush of color on Brianna's cheekbones was all the answer Eden needed. Her heart shattered into a million pieces then, the sorrow that stormed her so crushing she feared it would choke the air from her lungs.

"How the Fates must have laughed," she murmured in the deathly silence. "And how you must have *raged* when you realized you'd given birth to an ordinary girl. I'm sure it was only your aspiration to become the head of Hexa that stopped you from killing me that day. After all, who would appoint a callous leader prepared to take the life of her newborn child?"

Brianna paled.

"Eden," Malik warned, his voice fraught. "You don't—"

Brianna raised a hand, halting the Hexa agent.

"Is that what you really think of me?" she asked Eden in a low voice.

Eden blinked at the slight tremor underscoring her mother's words. Brianna's eyes had darkened with a nameless emotion. Eden swallowed and strengthened her resolve, determined to ignore the blatant lies of the woman opposite her.

"Yes. And don't worry. I am well aware how much everyone in Hexa hates me. That's why I can't do as you ask and go to a magic college, *mother*. I want to be rid of you all as soon as I become an adult." A mirthless chuckle left Eden at her mother's startled look. "To be honest, I thought you would be glad to see the back of me too. But it seems you are intent on torturing me for as long as you possibly can, all in the name of *caring* for me." She chortled again at the irony of the situation. "What a joke. You people wouldn't know the meaning of the word caring if it hit you in the face."

Laughter bubbled out of her. It rose and echoed around the room, turning loud and hysterical and full of pain.

It stopped abruptly when Brianna slapped her, the report so loud it sounded like a gun shot. An echo of her mother's magic rippled across the room and shook the books on the shelves.

Heat flared across Eden's left cheek, a sharp sting that brought her to her senses and seemed to last forever.

She raised a trembling hand to her throbbing face and stared at Brianna. "Finally."

Brianna gasped as Eden grabbed her manicured hand and brought it to her throat, a rictus distorting her features for a moment, as if she too were in pain.

"Do it, mother. I know it's what you've always wanted to do. Use your magic and squeeze the breath from my lungs." She moved Brianna's fingers to her chest, resisting her mother's attempt to yank her hand away. Her skin burned, as if Brianna's magic was scorching her. "Or better still, crush my heart. It will take you what, thirty to sixty seconds to kill me? No one will tell. After all, the people in this room are your faithful lackeys. I'm sure they'll be just as glad to gaze upon my lifeless corpse."

"Eden!" Valerie gasped.

"That's enough!" Malik barked.

"*You're grounded!*" Brianna roared, her eyes bright with fury and agony. She wrenched her hand from Eden's grasp.

The hot sensation abated. Eden gazed at her mother and saw a woman she knew only too well. One whose distraught expression shifted smoothly to the icy, dispassionate mask she loved to portray to the world.

"As of today, you will not step foot outside our home until I say so," Brianna continued, her voice as hard as steel. "I will ask your headteacher to give your homework to Malik. You will be allowed out in the garden for fresh air and exercise. That is all."

Brianna turned and walked around the desk.

Eden stared dully as her mother sat down and picked up the document she'd been reading, effectively dismissing her.

Malik took a careful hold of her elbow, his touch oddly gentle. "Let's go."

Eden allowed the Hexa agent to lead her to the exit.

She stopped on the threshold of the office, her heart pounding and her limbs heavy. She felt drained. Empty. As if she were a shell of a person. Malik frowned at her.

"Since we're finally being honest with one another, then let me tell you one last thing," Eden said quietly to the woman behind her. "Every day I wake up, I wish I had been born to any other woman but you."

Someone gasped, probably one of her mother's aides.

Eden walked out of the room with her head held high, conscious of the eyes on her back and the tense sorcerer at her side.

CHAPTER FIVE

CASSIUS WOKE UP TO A HEAVY ARM AROUND HIS WAIST and a hard chest pressed against his back. He carefully lifted his head off the pillow and glanced at the clock on the wall.

It was six a.m.

Since they'd wrapped up their latest case yesterday, he and Morgan didn't have to go into the office until late that morning. Cassius sighed, snuggled under the covers, and closed his eyes, determined to catch up on some much-needed Zs.

He was roused a while later by hot lips on his nape.

"Hmm," Cassius murmured drowsily. "We don't have to be up yet. Let's sleep some more."

Morgan nibbled on Cassius's ear and squeezed his body lightly.

Cassius sighed when he felt the solid erection nudging his butt, his torpor fading. "We had sex last night."

"Ah-huh."

Morgan shifted down the bed. Cassius shivered as the Aerial pressed scorching kisses down his spine.

"Three times," he stated half-accusingly.

"I'm not getting your point."

Morgan danced a hand along Cassius's waist and down his hip, his mouth busy on Cassius's back.

"I barely slept!" Cassius protested weakly.

"We can sleep when we're dead," Morgan declared confidently.

A soft gasp left Cassius when Morgan's fingers found his half-hard cock. It became a moan as Morgan started stroking him.

Morgan nipped at Cassius's shoulder with his teeth, his grip firm on his swelling flesh. "This part of you doesn't feel in the least bit sleepy."

"That's because you're—*oh fuck*—touching me!"

Cassius twitched and shuddered, now more than a little aroused. Loki sprang down from his favorite spot by his feet and padded out the bedroom, his tail swinging languorously.

Cassius writhed and panted on the bed as Morgan rubbed him briskly from behind. Morning sex with Morgan was always like this. Hot, fast, and screamingly good. Morgan's cock probed Cassius's cleft insistently as he pleasured him. The Aerial coated his fingers liberally with Cassius's precum before he opened his legs with his thigh and slipped two digits inside his still soft opening. Cassius cursed, his back passage clenching hungrily around Morgan.

Morgan rained kisses on Cassius's back as he thrust and scissored his fingers for breathless seconds, stretching him good before pulling out. Cassius moaned and gripped the pillow as Morgan entered him, head turning and hand rising to draw Morgan in for a kiss. Morgan took his mouth just the way he took his body, with strength and passion and heat enough to burn them both.

Pleasure stormed Cassius as they made love, Morgan's dick filling him to the brim over and over again, their pants and groans echoing around the bedroom. Morgan nudged the back of Cassius's knees up and adjusted the angle of penetration, his breaths hot and heavy on Cassius's neck, his fingers moving slickly on Cassius's aching cock.

"*Ah!*"

Light sparked across Cassius's vision when Morgan's shaft found his prostate. Incoherent sounds left him as Morgan pounded his sweet spot, his dick spurting out precum over Morgan's fingers in tandem with each thrust. Fire ignited between their soul cores, making them gasp.

"You feel *SO* good!" Morgan groaned. "I could stay inside you all day!"

It wasn't long before they climaxed, Cassius shouting out as he came. Morgan shuddered and grunted behind him, teeth sinking into Cassius's shoulder and hips pumping his throbbing length fitfully inside Cassius's body as he ejaculated. Cassius bit his lip, relishing the sweetly savage sensation.

It was some time before they came down from their high, their bodies slick with sweat and their hearts racing. Morgan pulled out of Cassius, grabbed some wipes, and carefully cleaned him down. He disposed of the tissues before lying on his back and rolling Cassius atop him.

"That was a great wake-up call," he murmured in Cassius's hair.

Cassius couldn't garner the energy to protest, his cheek hot where it kissed Morgan's chest, the strong heartbeat beneath a familiar lullaby that soothed his soul.

"How about we play hooky and skip work today?" Morgan suggested.

"Adrianne will have our balls if we do that," Cassius mumbled. "Besides, I want to check the archives again."

Morgan nuzzled Cassius's locks with his lips. "You still haven't given up on that?"

Cassius lifted his head and frowned at Morgan. "You mean finding out about Ivmir? No, I haven't. And neither should you."

Morgan sighed. "I didn't mean it like that. A lot has happened since you came to San Francisco and you're only just settling into the city and my team. That information will still be there a few months from now, if it exists."

Cassius pursed his lips. "I know. But I can't help but feel that what went down with Chester is just the beginning of something bigger. And that the sooner we recover our memories and powers, the more prepared we will be for whatever that is."

Morgan was silent for a while.

"London may hold some answers," he said quietly. "Their Argonaut archives are the oldest in the world.

So are the historical records of the other agencies based there."

Cassius hesitated. London was where Victor Sloan, his former lover and the current head of Cabalista, was based. Victor was supposed to visit San Francisco three weeks ago but had cancelled at the last moment, a local situation requiring his attention. Cassius had been half-relieved. He knew Victor would immediately guess the nature of the relationship between him and Morgan if he saw them together. It didn't help that Morgan grew territorial in the presence of any male he deemed to be interested in Cassius.

Maybe I should have him on a leash.

Cassius swallowed a smile at the thought of putting a lead on Morgan. Desire stirred inside him when his imagination went rampant, images of tying the Aerial to his bed and doing all kinds of wicked things to him making his belly clench with another wave of lust.

Morgan's hands found Cassius's butt when he felt his fresh arousal. He fondled his ass and thrust up, his thickening cock sliding against Cassius's swelling erection. Cassius inhaled raggedly as Morgan parted his cheeks with his fingers.

Their phones buzzed with an incoming text.

Morgan stilled.

"That had better be something important," he grumbled.

He slid out from under Cassius, grabbed his cell from the floor, and stared at the screen.

A heavy frown wrinkled his brow. "You seeing the same message I am?"

"About an urgent meeting?" Cassius narrowed his eyes at his phone display. "Yeah."

The missive had come directly from Strickland. Their entire team had been ordered to attend his office at 8 a.m. on the dot.

"I have a bad feeling," Morgan muttered.

Cassius looked at him uneasily. "What kind of bad feeling?"

"The kind that says we're gonna be working all kinds of stupid hours from today and I'm not gonna be able to have my fill of you."

Cassius threw a pillow at the sulking angel.

CHAPTER SIX

"This is Detective Sergeant Holly Lambert and Detective Inspector Barry Willis from the San Francisco PD Central Investigations Bureau, Major Crimes Task Force."

Morgan studied the bright-eyed woman and somber man observing them steadily from across the coffee table while Strickland introduced his team. Lambert looked to be in her early forties, while Willis was skirting his fifties. Both detectives straightened slightly when Cassius's name came up.

"So, you're the famous Cassius Black," Willis said impassively.

Lambert smiled. "Nice to meet you, Mr. Black. Rumor has it you played an integral part in saving our collective bacon a month ago from a nasty warlock."

"He did?" Willis said, shocked.

Strickland narrowed his eyes.

Morgan sympathized with the director. Their clash

with Chester Moran was meant to be a closely guarded secret. Outside of the supernatural agencies, the mayor and the Chief of Police were the only other people who had been made aware of what had gone down beneath the cathedral on Nob Hill.

Lambert sighed. "This is exactly why I said you should start hanging out with us at the bar more often, Barry."

"You know I'm a teetotaler," Willis protested.

"They serve non-alcoholic drinks." Lambert registered their cool stares. "Anyway, we should get down to business. We're here because we need Argonaut's help. Our Deputy Chief approached Director Strickland yesterday and he agreed to assign you guys to our case."

Morgan stared at Strickland. "Did he now?"

Strickland ignored his pointed look. The director normally discussed all their cases with him before they were officially allocated to his team.

"Why does San Francisco PD need our assistance?" Adrianne asked curiously.

Willis glanced at Lambert. The senior detective nodded.

"We're currently working on a spate of break-ins that have taken place across the city in the last two weeks," Willis said. "They all involve banks."

"Oh." Bailey blinked. "You mean the 'Sock Them and Knock Them' raids?"

Lambert frowned faintly at the wizard. "Where did you hear that term?"

Bailey shrugged. "Hey, you're not the only people with the means to access other organizations' insider information." He leaned toward Zach, his voice dropping to a conspiratorial whisper. "I heard it from one of the bartenders at *Occulta*."

The demon sighed. He was currently dating Suzie Myers, the owner of *Occulta,* the number one place to hang out in San Francisco if you were a magic user or otherworldly. Suzie was a Level One witch who had helped them out during the Chester Moran affair.

Cassius glanced between the detectives. "Why 'Sock Them and Knock Them?'"

Lambert grimaced and rubbed the back of her neck. "Because it's the characteristic modus operandi of our perps. All nine robberies have involved the guards being knocked out by an explosive device of sorts and the bank vault doors being wrenched off their hinges as if a wrecking ball has smashed into them. We're pretty sure it's the same people behind all break-ins. Intelligence chatter hasn't revealed any clues so far and no criminal organization is behaving out of the norm at the moment, so we're completely in the dark as to who they are."

Morgan leaned his elbows on his knees, growing impatient. "What does Argonaut have to do with any of this?"

"Our police commander told us there were faint traces of magic at the scene of one of the crimes," Lambert replied.

Surprise darted through Morgan.

Adrianne raised an eyebrow. "Your police commander?"

"You mean Jessica Kessler?" Strickland asked Lambert brusquely.

"Yes. I take it from your expression that you know her?"

"I do. She has a bit of magic in her soul core, but that shouldn't give her the ability to detect magical remains." Strickland frowned. "Her husband, on the other hand, is a Level Five mage working for Hexa."

Lambert dipped her head. "You're correct. It was Armand Kessler who picked up the scent of magic that lingered on his wife after she visited one of the banks."

"These burglaries are not ordinary," Willis continued. "Though items of value have gone missing from the vaults, a lot of expensive stuff was just left lying around. It's as if the people behind the robberies are stealing random junk to hide their true intentions."

"Steady there, Barry," Lambert murmured. "One of those pieces of junk is worth five million dollars." She waved a vague hand at their inquisitive looks. "A diamond tiara worn by some fifteenth century European queen."

Cassius frowned. "You think they're looking for something specific?"

"I do. It's the only thing that makes sense. And there's something else." Lambert exchanged a troubled look with Willis. "The security recordings from the time of the break-ins have all been destroyed."

"Destroyed?" Julia repeated. "You mean, the banks' security systems were hacked?"

"Yes and no. As you probably know, all banks maintain physical backups of their camera feeds at a secure off-site location. Not only were their local files isolated and erased, the remote data centers where the recordings were being kept malfunctioned and lost all the information on those particular drives."

"The witness accounts we have are pretty limited," Willis continued. "Every guard present at the time of the burglaries lost consciousness before they saw any of the perps."

"What about the street cameras around the banks?" Adrianne asked. "Surely they must have caught something when the robberies happened."

Lambert shook her head. "We got nothing from them. It's as if these guys are ghosts."

Morgan sensed an echo of unease from Cassius. "What is it?"

Cassius stared blindly at the floor. "If it's something specific they're after and magic is involved, then it might be an artifact of sorts."

Morgan stiffened, the reason behind Cassius's apprehension now clear.

Chester Moran had been after the Eternity Key, an artifact reputed to have locked Chaos in the Abyss. The current Keeper of the Key had turned out to be none other than Loki, Cassius's newly adopted cat, an imp who had taken the form of an animal so as to hide on Earth.

It had become clear to Cassius, Morgan, and the supernatural agencies during that incident that the person who had manipulated Chester Moran from behind the scenes was the same one who had similarly orchestrated Tania Lancaster's reign of terror over Europe and England half a century ago. Chester had turned out to be Tania's son and had fallen prey to the same madness that had gripped his mother.

Morgan masked a shiver as he recalled the voice they had heard in the cave where Chester had met his death. The being who had possessed Chester's corpse had spoken as if he knew Cassius and Morgan from before the Fall. Morgan suspected Cassius was still haunted by their enemy's words.

The man had insinuated that he had used Cassius to his advantage in the past and was responsible for all the misery that had befallen the Empyreal.

Morgan knew he hadn't lied. He had felt the dark truth of the enemy's statement in the very marrow of his bones, just as Cassius had done when his eyes had filled with sudden tears in the midst of battle. Morgan would never forgive the man who had hurt Cassius, before and after the Fall. His nails dug into his palms.

He will die by my hand.

"We've examined the records of what was stored in those vaults ad nauseam," Lambert said with a faint frown. "Nothing stood out in particular."

"Magical artifacts tend not to be obvious," Cassius said. "And if the burglaries are still happening, that means the perpetrators have yet to find what they're looking for."

"As of now, Morgan and his team are at your disposal," Strickland told the two detectives. "Keep me informed of any developments," the director added for

Morgan's benefit. He hesitated and studied Cassius with a troubled expression. "Let me know if you detect any presence of black magic during your investigation. We need to bring the other agencies in the loop if we suspect the man who manipulated Chester is behind this. I'm not making the same mistake I made last month."

CHAPTER SEVEN

THE NOISE OF THE MID-MORNING TRAFFIC ON MARKET Street rushed over Cassius as he stepped out of the SUV. He shrugged into his Argonaut jacket and joined Morgan and the rest of their team on the sidewalk. A high rise loomed before them, one of dozens in the city's financial district.

A police cordon was in place in front of the bank's main entrance. A security guard supported by two San Francisco PD officers was checking in everyone going inside the building. The cops waved Lambert and Willis through when they spotted the detectives, their curious gazes dancing briefly over the Argonaut agents in their wake.

They entered the main hall of the bank.

"Anyone sensing anything unusual yet?" Morgan asked quietly as they crossed the marble floor.

Murmured 'no's rose from their group.

Bailey grimaced. "All I smell is gunpowder."

"I think I...feel something," Charlie mumbled.

Morgan slowed and stared at the enchanter. "What is it?"

Charlie hesitated. "The remnants of an enchantment spell. It's very faint."

Morgan's gaze switched to Cassius.

"He's right," Cassius murmured. "I can detect a trace of magic." He paused. "Armand Kessler must be a powerful mage to have picked this up on his wife's clothes."

The public area of the bank occupied over half the first floor of the building. The rest of it and the floors above them were dedicated to the offices of the bank, while the main vault and the boiler rooms took up most of the basement.

Lambert and Willis headed past the information desk and made for a thick, steel-reinforced, metal security door hanging crookedly on its frame near the back of the hall. Two officers were guarding the doorway.

Cassius and the others slowed to inspect the damage.

Parts of the panel had melted under whatever explosive the perpetrators had used, while the rest was crushed and distorted due to percussive energy.

Adrianne squatted and traced a finger across a dark residue coating the door. She sniffed it and frowned before straightening and dusting off her hands.

"All I'm getting is gunpowder. Which is strange."

"Why so?" Lambert asked impassively.

"There are more potent and stable compounds than gunpowder out there these days," Zach said. "Makes you wonder why these guys are using it."

Lambert nodded, clearly pleased with their observations. "Our explosive experts found that strange too. It's the same at all the crime scenes."

The detectives had yet to share their case files with them. Morgan had agreed it would be best for his team to approach the investigation with an unbiased perspective.

Lambert led the way down the corridor beyond the damaged door. They navigated a couple of turns and reached a lift with a biometric data panel. Surprise danced through Cassius when it opened without taking anyone's retinal scan or fingerprints.

Lambert smiled faintly at his expression. "The bank disabled the secure access. You'll see why when we get to the basement."

They emerged into a brightly lit underground chamber seconds later.

"Wow," Bailey muttered. "Someone had fun down here."

Lambert made a face. "I think the insurance company would disagree. It's going to cost millions to fix this place."

The basement was milling with cops and security staff. Cassius saw why it would be pointless to get everyone security access before they could come down here. It would only end up losing the detectives precious time and delay their investigation.

The vandalized vault door dominated the foyer, the deformed circular hatch with its complex locks and bolts tilting precariously on its melted hinges. They examined it before heading inside the strongroom.

Safety deposit boxes lay strewn across the floor, their precious contents discarded like so much flotsam. The robbers had ignored the gold bars and bullion stacked inside the secondary vault at the far end of the chamber and focused their attention on the strongboxes instead.

It was an hour before they finished going over the room. Bar the gunpowder smell, they didn't detect anything, much to Lambert and Willis's chagrin. They returned to the first floor and were making plans to visit the next crime scene when Cassius slowed and stopped.

Morgan halted in his tracks. "What is it?"

They were halfway across the main hall.

Cassius's gaze swept their surroundings. "I'm…not sure."

He could feel the magic he and Charlie had detected before. There was something else. Something almost intangible in the air he hadn't picked up before. A scent he couldn't quite identify. He dropped on his haunches and pressed his palm against the marble.

To his surprise, it felt warm to the touch. Cassius clenched his jaw.

That's magic alright.

"Was this the last place that got broken into?" he asked the detectives tensely.

"Yeah," Willis replied. "It's the crime scene with the freshest evidence, so we thought it best to bring you guys here first. This break-in happened two days ago."

"You made the right call," Cassius murmured. He rose and slowly retraced his steps, his gaze on the floor. "The guards who were present at the time were knocked out by an explosion?"

Lambert and Willis exchanged a puzzled glance.

"Yes," Lambert said. "We already told you that."

Cassius stopped next to the information desk. He ignored the anxious looks of the people manning it and observed the area carefully before gazing up at the ceiling. "How badly were they injured?"

"They were lucky for the most part." Willis shrugged. "There were a few broken bones and some minor burns."

Cassius glanced at the detectives. "You guys didn't find that kinda strange?" He indicated the damaged security door leading to the vault. "Looking at that, anybody in the vicinity who wasn't behind a defensive magic shield should have been toast. But then again, considering the lack of damage to the rest of this room, it's clear they didn't use a normal explosive device."

The cops framing the doorway exchanged nervous looks.

Lambert narrowed her eyes. "What are you getting at?"

"Your guards weren't knocked out by a bomb. They had a spell placed on them." Cassius squatted and touched the floor again. He frowned. "One that was some time in the making." He looked over his shoulder. "Bailey, Adrianne, I need you. You too, Charlie."

The enchanter fell into step behind the wizard and the sorceress, surprised. Cassius straightened.

"Can you clear the area?" he asked Lambert and Willis. "This might get a little dangerous."

CHAPTER EIGHT

It took several minutes to empty the place of human onlookers. Cassius had the two detectives and police officers step inside the corridor beyond the security door.

"It would be best if you close your eyes and cover your ears," he told them. "This spell may be weak but it could still affect you."

Lambert didn't look happy about his request.

"We need to see this," Willis said stubbornly.

Cassius sighed. He could tell he wasn't going to be able to convince the detectives. "Bailey, shield them."

Light flared in Bailey's right hand. The wizard cast a magic orb toward the doorway. The sphere expanded into a translucent, wavering wall as it sailed through the air. It blocked the opening, sealing the cops off from any magic that might harm them.

"Shouldn't we be behind that too?" Julia said.

Cassius shook his head. "We need to experience this

at close range. It might tell us more about our perps." He looked at Adrianne. "Can you cast a reversal spell right here?" He pointed at the ground. "Bailey, get ready to slow it down the second it activates. Charlie, focus on what you're sensing once Adrianne reverses the spell. I suspect you'll be the only one who can detect its true origin."

Adrianne and Bailey removed their rune-covered daggers from their belts. Brightness flared on the blades as they poured magic into them, illuminating the symbols.

"Can't you just skip the Holmes act and tell us what you think is going on?" the sorceress muttered, placing the tip of her weapon on the floor.

"It's better if we see it with our own eyes," Cassius said stubbornly.

Bailey exchanged a wary look with Adrianne.

The scent of Valerian filled the air as the sorceress unleashed the reversal spell. The aroma of Frankincense followed from Bailey's soul core.

Sparks danced across the marble from Adrianne's dagger. They merged, forming lines on the floor that mapped out a conjuration that had been invisible to the naked eye.

"Bloody hellfire!" Adrianne gasped.

A wave of magic rippled across the hall as the spell activated. Heat and noise detonated over them.

"*Now!*" Cassius barked at Bailey.

Bailey stabbed his blade next to Adrianne's.

The explosion blooming into existence in the

middle of the room decelerated. A familiar pulse of power throbbed through the air and washed across Cassius's skin in the next instant.

"Cassius!" Morgan barked, closing in on them.

"We're okay." Cassius's gaze remained locked on the slow-moving phenomenon. "It's not real."

"It looks real enough from here!" Morgan growled.

Charlie gasped.

Cassius looked at the enchanter before following his unblinking gaze to the ceiling. An infinitesimal glimmer caught his eye. He extended his wings and shot up into the air. The scent he couldn't define earlier was now clear.

Cassius unsheathed his dagger, released his Stark Steel sword, and sent a pulse of seraphic energy through it. He swung the blade in a swooping diagonal arc at the area in front of him.

Metal clanged and sparks erupted as his sword struck something invisible. Cassius frowned and unleashed another wave of seraphic energy.

Static exploded next to his blade. A small, dark, spinning metal cube materialized, the spell shielding it weakened by Cassius's blade and power. It fitted neatly into his palm as he took hold of it, the box throbbing and vibrating warmly in his grasp.

Cassius dropped to the ground.

Adrianne and Bailey had ended the spell reversal. Everyone gathered around Cassius, Lambert and Willis joining them swiftly once Bailey's barrier had dissipated.

"What the heck did we just see?" the senior detective said grimly.

"An enchantment," Cassius murmured. "One designed to mimic an explosion."

Charlie had grown pale. He took the cube from Cassius, his hands trembling slightly. Cassius wasn't surprised.

He didn't need to be a genius to recognize how complex this whole setup was.

"Wait." Willis frowned. "You're saying the guards were really knocked out by that enchantment? But they had injuries. An enchantment can't do that!"

"The perpetrators probably knocked them about while they were bewitched." Admiration gleamed in Morgan's gaze as he looked at Cassius. "How did you know?"

"This crime scene doesn't obey the laws of physics or standard destructive magic spells," Cassius said with a faint frown. "Plus, I could smell something else apart from gunpowder just now. It was cedar. It resonated with Charlie's magic."

The scent wafting off the cube was redolent of the powers of an enchanter.

Lambert frowned. "What about that security door and the vault room? A spell wouldn't do that level of damage to metal."

"They definitely used bombs for that," Cassius said with a firm dip of his chin. "Whatever the explosive was, it's non-standard."

"Non-standard?" Willis repeated, puzzled.

"Not used by humans," Zach explained.

"We should take some samples of the damaged metal and send them to Maggie," Cassius told Morgan.

Maggie Briggs was the head of forensics at Argonaut and a witch. If anyone could tell them the ingredients of the mysterious explosive, it was her.

Morgan nodded.

"So magic users were behind these robberies all along?" Lambert said between gritted teeth.

"Yeah," Cassius said apologetically. "But you couldn't have known. They did a good job masking their tracks."

Bailey stared at the cube in Charlie's hands. "What the heck is this thing anyway?"

"I don't know." Cassius studied the enchanter steadily. "I'm hoping Charlie can tell us."

"It's an Altered Mind box," Charlie said in a low voice.

Adrianne made a face. "What's an Altered Mind box?"

Morgan scowled. "Shit!"

Cassius stared at him. "You've heard of it?"

"Yeah." A muscle jumped in Morgan's cheek. "Rumors of it started circulating among our intelligence agents a few months ago. It's a new device that combines cutting-edge, virtual-reality technology and magic."

"Morgan's right." Concern clouded Charlie's eyes as he gazed at the tiny box. "Someone I know said they'd seen one being used at a private club in L.A. It put everyone under an enchantment where they were able to experience mass sex. And I don't mean just in their minds. It was physical too."

"Wait," Bailey said dully. "Someone invented a magic VR cube that can simulate orgies?"

Adrianne narrowed her eyes at the wizard.

"Hey, I'm just repeating what I'm hearing," Bailey muttered defensively.

"Why the devil would somebody go to all this trouble?" Lambert said with a scowl. "Why not use standard enchantments or normal explosives?"

"An Altered Mind box can be used over and over again and not drain the enchanter," Charlie explained. "It can also be timed to go off on a specific schedule."

"I'm afraid your suspicions were correct," Morgan told Lambert and Willis in a hard voice. "Whoever these people are, they didn't want to be seen and they definitely didn't want to be traced."

"Had they used obvious magic from the get-go, this case would have come under our jurisdiction and they wouldn't have been able to move as freely as they've done these past weeks," Cassius added. "Which means whatever they're after has to be extremely valuable or powerful and they don't want anyone in the supernatural or magical community to know about it."

Morgan frowned at Cassius. "Can you feel any black magic on this thing?"

"No," Cassius replied reluctantly. "This doesn't feel like what we encountered when we faced Chester and his sorcerers."

Disquiet danced through him. Despite the lack of

black magic, he couldn't help but feel that this was connected to Chester and Tania's master. His instincts had been right too many times in the past for him to ignore them.

They had to secure whatever these bank robbers were after before they found it.

CHAPTER NINE

EDEN FROZE, ONE LEG OVER THE WINDOWSILL OF HER bedroom. She studied the area below her, mouth dry and heart thumping violently against her ribs.

The guard patrolling the backyard was standing some thirty feet beneath her. He was gazing out over the dark, landscaped gardens that dropped down from the rear patio, the swimming pool a bright rectangle of light at the bottom of the incline. Eden swallowed.

By her calculations, the guard should have finished his rounds of this area of the property by now.

The man finally moved. Eden waited a full minute after he'd disappeared around the corner of the mansion before carefully clambering down the wall, the corbels and quoins adorning the facade of the building providing ample support for her feet and hands. Having tested out the path of her descent before, she knew how to get to the ground safely.

She landed lightly on the terrace and was about to head down into the gardens when a figure materialized to her left. Eden froze where she crouched, the carbon-nanotube reflective cloak she wore rustling ever so faintly in a mild breeze. She cursed silently and gripped the folds to stop them from moving, her eyes focused unblinkingly on the man fifteen feet from her.

Great. It had to be him, of all people.

Malik's gaze locked on her position. A faint frown marred the Hexa sorcerer's brow.

Please, please, *don't use your magic!*

The cloak Eden had purchased through her best friend would be able to hide her from normal eyes, but a magic user might still detect her.

Malik stayed still for a moment before strolling past her and heading around the side of the mansion.

Eden blew out a sigh and sent a silent thanks to the Heavens.

She moved nimbly down the stone steps leading into the gardens, skirted the swimming pool, and found the narrow gap in the hedge that separated her home from her neighbor down the hill.

Wesley, the elderly bulldog that ruled over the backyard of the next property, shuffled into view as Eden squeezed through the bushes. A low whine escaped the dog. Eden hushed him, slipped a hand inside one of the pockets of her camo pants, and extracted the hotdog she'd brought for him from a sandwich bag.

Wesley gulped it down in two bites and licked her hand.

Eden petted the dog before heading for the side gate. She navigated the narrow path that ran between the properties straddling the block and came out onto the next street.

Eden studied the dark road to make sure it was clear, turned left, and made her way swiftly toward the towering trees rising in the distance. It took but seconds to scale the metal fence and enter the vast park that took up the northwest portion of the city.

Leaves rustled above her as she moved in the darkness. She cut across Presidio Boulevard, took a trail heading south, and was soon in Presidio Heights.

The scent of jasmine and roses teased her nostrils as she approached the pretty, red-brick Georgian house where her best friend lived. The place was as different from Eden's home as the sun was from the moon. She walked quietly past the neat front yard with its trellises and borders full of colorful flowers, climbed over the side gate, and entered the rear garden.

Pale light shone out of one of the windows on the second floor. Eden grabbed two acorns from the ground and cast them carefully at the glass. A shadow appeared a few seconds later.

Wood creaked softly in the night as Lois Serrano pulled up the sash window. Eden drew the hood of the cloak back. Her best friend's eyes widened when she saw her.

"You made it!" she whispered fiercely, her voice full of equal dread and excitement.

Eden smiled, relief making her almost weak. She couldn't believe her plan had actually worked.

I couldn't have done it without Lo.

Lois rolled a rope down the wall and helped Eden

climb up. Eden laughed as she tumbled into her best friend's arms and took her to the floor.

"*Ssssh!*" Lois hushed her. "You'll wake my parents!"

"Sorry," Eden mumbled in between chuckles and snorts.

She knew her laughter was driven by hysteria. She'd just run away from home. Not that she could ever call that place a real home.

Lois rose to her feet, yanked her up, and pulled her into her arms. "Are you okay?"

Eden shuddered and closed her eyes as she hugged her friend fiercely. "Yeah. I am now."

Lois dragged her over to the bed. They sat on the edge of the mattress, Lois holding Eden's hand and running her thumb anxiously over Eden's knuckles.

"Are you sure about this, Edie?"

Eden smiled faintly at the nickname. "Yes."

Lois had called her Edie and Eden had called her Lo for as long as she could remember. They'd met when they were in kindergarten and had been best friends since. Lois was the closest thing to a sister Eden had and the only one she'd ever felt able to confide in over the years as the distance between her and Brianna had grown into a chasm she knew she could never cross. Though she came from a non-magical family, Lois had sympathized with Eden's plight and been a pillar of support for her even after Brianna forcefully enrolled her at Saint Helena High.

When Eden first told her of the plan she wanted to put in place to escape Brianna's clutches if worse came to worse, Lois had done her best to dissuade her, too scared of what Eden was proposing to see the logic of the scheme. She'd finally given in after much convincing and had helped Eden gather the resources and tools she would need to survive until she found a safe place to stay.

Luckily, money wasn't an issue. Eden had a generous savings account, courtesy of her mother. The fake ID documents and high school diploma she'd purchased off the dark web had cost her a pretty penny but had allowed her to open a new bank account online, where she'd transferred most of her savings. Eden had no qualms about using her mother's money. After everything Brianna had put her through, she deserved the paycheck.

She hadn't told Lois that she had found somewhere she wanted to go a few months ago. There was a farm with extensive orchards outside San Diego looking for people to help out for most of the year. Eden had always wanted to live in the country and working on a farm sounded like the kind of grueling physical labor that would keep her busy while she figured out what she wanted to do with the rest of her life. She had already sent in her application for them to consider her and they had provisionally given her an offer of work.

Lois worried her lip with her teeth. "Do you know where you're gonna stay tonight?"

"Yeah. I booked a place in town from tomorrow. I'm planning to stay there a couple of nights before traveling south."

Eden knew her mother and Hexa would scour the transport hubs in and around San Francisco in the next twenty-four hours in an attempt to find her. They wouldn't expect her to stay in the city for a few days while the search was on.

"What about tonight?" Lois looked around her bedroom. "Just stay here. There's plenty of space!"

Eden shook her head, her expression turning sad. "This is the first place my mom will come to when she finds out I'm missing. I won't put you or your family at risk."

Lois hesitated before reluctantly dipping her head. She rose and got a large travel backpack from her closet. It was full of camping gear, survival tools, and energy bars, as well as a few changes of clothes and toiletries.

She helped Eden lower it into the garden and stood hesitantly at the window, her face pale and her eyes glimmering with tears. "Will I see you again?"

Eden sniffed and wiped her own eyes, her heart twisting with regret and pain. She hated leaving Lois. Her mother's face swam before her, bringing with it a wave of bitter resentment.

I loathe her SO much!

"I'll write when it's safe," she mumbled.

Lois nodded shakily. She gave Eden a fierce hug before helping her down the wall.

Eden hefted the backpack onto her shoulders and cast a final look at her best friend before heading out the rear gate. She intended to spend the night in the park and make her way into the city the next day.

She'd just turned the corner of the next street over

when a faint whiff of rotting meat danced across her nostrils.

Eden whipped around, her knuckles whitening on the straps of her backpack.

The night was still, the sound of traffic from the neighboring main roads faint. Nothing stirred in the darkness. She hesitated before making her way swiftly toward the park, blaming her overactive imagination.

CHAPTER TEN

Brianna blinked her eyes open. The clock on her nightstand came into focus. She sighed when she saw the time.

It had just gone three a.m.

Well, two hours is better than nothing.

She rolled onto her back and covered her face with her arm, knowing sleep would evade her for the rest of the night. The heated exchange she'd had with Eden yesterday played through her mind for the hundredth time.

Was I wrong to keep my distance?

Brianna clenched her jaw, her stomach twisting with sorrow and guilt as she recalled Eden's lifeless face at the end of their fight. The words her daughter had spoken in the heat of their argument had not been lies. That Eden hated her and Hexa and detested her life to the point she would rather be dead had still come as a shock. Brianna had done everything in her power to give Eden a comfortable life over the last sixteen years. The only thing she hadn't been able to bestow freely upon her daughter was her love and affection. And she'd had little choice in that matter.

Eden's soul core was still unstable, despite the spell that had imprisoned it since her birth. The cursed magic within would be deadly if it were to be released from its chains. Even now, it reacted aggressively to Brianna's magic, as if it knew she was the one responsible for holding it captive for all these years. Any physical contact between them triggered its rage. In the past, this had caused Eden and Brianna immense physical pain, to the point Eden would often faint. It was in desperation that the Hexa mages had suggested Brianna physically distance herself from her daughter, for both their sakes.

It was the only way she could keep Eden safe and protect those around them from her daughter's destructive magic.

Brianna gripped the bedsheet, frustration gnawing at her. Had she known when she and the Hexa mages had bound Eden's fragile and dangerous life force hours after she was born that it would mean she couldn't touch her own daughter for years to come without crippling pain for both of them, she might not have made the same decision she did that fateful night. She swallowed then, bitterness filling her veins at the thought.

Who am I kidding? I would do it all over again to save her.

Brianna's heart grew heavy. She had always wanted a child. In fact, she had wanted several children. So had the sorcerer she had fallen in love with during the magical summer she'd spent in Paris twenty years ago, when she was apprenticing at the Hexa bureau there. It had taken them several years to conceive and those years had been the most blissful of Brianna's life, though she hadn't known it at the time. Her pregnancy when it came had been welcomed with tears and she'd looked breathlessly forward to the day she would hold her and her husband's child in her arms.

It wasn't until her second trimester that things started to go wrong.

Brianna frowned and sat up. She didn't want to relive those painful memories again. She got out of bed and poured herself a glass of water from the carafe on the nightstand.

Her wandering footsteps soon took her to her daughter's bedroom.

Brianna took a shallow breath and carefully opened the door. The illumination from the security lights in the garden painted a pale strip on the ceiling and walls of Eden's room. Brianna's gaze found the shape under the covers in the bed to her left.

Movement up ahead drew her gaze. The curtains at one of the windows overlooking the garden fluttered slightly in a mild night breeze, bringing a chill to the air. She crossed the bedroom quietly and closed the window. She cast a final, longing look at her daughter's sleeping form and was almost at the door when she froze in her tracks, her subconscious finally registering what her soul core was screaming at her.

She couldn't feel the hot, stabbing pain she

normally experienced deep inside her body when she was physically close to Eden. Fear gripped Brianna. She whirled around, stormed to the bed, and yanked the covers back.

The two pillows lying in the middle of the mattress seemed to mock her.

The glass fell from her hand and clattered to the floor, spilling cold water across her bare feet.

No!

Eden wasn't sure what roused her. The sleeping bag rustled faintly as she shifted onto her side and sat up. She frowned sleepily at her watch, the luminous dials pale in the gloom. It was an hour before dawn.

She stayed still and listened, tension swirling slowly through her.

Did they find me?!

Bar the rush of waves in the distance and the wind whispering in the trees, she heard nothing. She relaxed.

The spot she'd chosen to camp out at was located in a thick coppice not far from Baker Beach. It was over two miles from her house and desolate at this time of day.

Eden knew she would have to make herself scarce by sunrise. A lot of runners used the nearby trails in the morning. The last thing she needed was to bring any unnecessary attention to herself; being found sleeping in a tent under the trees was bound to do just that.

She was about to lie down again when a faint grunt sounded somewhere close by. Eden stiffened, senses on high alert.

It hadn't sounded human.

She swallowed and gripped the flashlight next to her. It was the best weapon she had on her, bar the Swiss Army knife in her pocket. She suppressed a grimace.

She didn't exactly want to use it on something alive.

Maybe it's a coyote. Or a deer.

The noise of a scuffle reached Eden. Apprehension paralyzed her.

It was a moment before she found the courage to move.

She slipped out of her sleeping bag, started sliding the tent fastener down, and froze when it made a faint swishing noise. She bit her lip and undid it at a slower pace. Cool, salty air danced through the slit-like opening. She peered one eye through it.

Her vision slowly adapted to the gloom. The dark shapes of tightly packed trees emerged from the shadows.

There was no one there.

Eden hesitated before carefully crawling outside. She rose into a low crouch and moved around the tent, her sock-covered feet silent on the grass.

The reflective cloak shivered in the breeze where she'd hung it on some low branches. It masked the tent's presence from the east, where the sun would reveal its location first. She advanced cautiously across the ground and peered around the edge of the material.

The guttural sound came again. Her gaze swung to the west.

For a fleeting second, she thought she saw two shapes next to some bushes. She blinked.

Whatever she thought she'd seen was gone.

Eden stayed motionless and gazed warily into the darkness until the sky started to lighten, her heart thumping a rapid beat in her chest.

It wasn't until the sun peeked above the horizon that she finally returned to the tent. She packed up, folded everything into the bag, and hoisted it onto her shoulders. By the time she crossed the carpark a short distance from where she'd camped, the first joggers had appeared.

CHAPTER ELEVEN

DREAD TWISTED BRIANNA'S STOMACH AS SHE STARED AT the front door of the Serranos' home. It was ajar, lock broken and light from the rising sun stabbing pale fingers through the shadows in the hallway. The scent of blood carried faintly on the breeze.

No one had answered when Brianna had called the landline a while back. Lois Serrano's cellphone had similarly yielded no response. After searching the area around the mansion for Eden and finding no traces of her daughter, this was the first place Brianna had thought to come to.

The premonition that had been tickling her subconscious for the last hour had borne fruit. Something had happened to the Serranos. Brianna had no doubt it was linked to her daughter's disappearance in some way.

She signaled to Malik and the Hexa agents who had accompanied her. They stormed the building silently, weapons drawn and magic muffling their footsteps.

Whoever the enemy was who'd attacked the Serranos, they were long gone.

They found Gary and Helen Serrano upstairs in the hallway, outside their children's bedrooms. Blood was congealing under their bodies, staining the parquet floor a dark brown. They were unconscious but still breathing.

The Hexa medical mage who'd accompanied Brianna started healing the jagged wounds carved into their flesh, magic shimmering around his hands.

Brianna found Lois in her little brother's bedroom. The girl was curled protectively around her sibling, the slashes on her back, arms, and legs telling the stark story of how she'd shielded him with her body during the savage assault.

Josh Serrano lay shivering under his sister's limp form, face pale, eyes glazed and unseeing with shock. The five-year-old had wet himself and was clinging to Lois with white-knuckled fingers.

"Josh?" Brianna said softly as she carefully approached them.

The little boy startled violently and whimpered.

"Ssssh," Brianna whispered, her heart clenching at his obvious terror. "It's okay, sweetie. I'm not gonna hurt you."

A muscle jumped in Malik's cheek where he stood at the threshold of the room. "Is she alive?"

Brianna laid a hand on Lois's back. She swallowed and closed her eyes briefly, relief swamping her when she felt the girl's shallow breaths.

"Yes."

Lois's life force still thrummed strongly through her veins despite the blood she'd lost.

"Bring the medical mage," Brianna said, anger making her tone hard.

Malik disappeared, his expression haggard.

Brianna knew the sorcerer blamed himself for having let Eden escape. Whatever she said to him wouldn't alleviate his guilt at what had happened here tonight. Lois had been a familiar figure at Eden and Brianna's home. Brianna knew the Hexa agents liked the young girl and regarded her with the same respect they did her daughter.

It seemed Eden had been determined to flee the prison she thought she'd been trapped in all her life and had sought her best friend's help to do so. Brianna had no one but herself to hold accountable for making her daughter think that way.

By the time ambulances turned up to take the Serranos to the hospital, Lois's father had regained consciousness.

"What happened?" Gary Serrano mumbled weakly to Brianna as he was being wheeled outside his home.

He was the last one out, the vehicles carrying his wife and daughter already en route to the hospital.

The Serranos' neighbors were out on the street and staring avidly at the developing situation, most in their housecoats and pajamas still. Several of the Serranos' close friends were arguing with the Hexa agents manning the security cordons that had been set up around the property, demanding to be allowed through to check on the children.

"You were attacked," Brianna told Gary somberly.

Tense voices drew her gaze to the left. Two San Francisco PD officers and a detective were having a taut discussion with Malik.

Panic drained the color from Gary's face. He grabbed Brianna's hand. "My wife?! Our children?!"

"They're safe. Helen and Lois were injured, but my mages healed most of their wounds. Josh is with your sister."

Relief had Gary sagging on the stretcher. "Thank you!" His expression grew distracted. "Our health insurance. I have to get the paperwork."

Brianna squeezed his fingers. "Don't worry about that. Hexa will be picking up the bill for what happened to you and your family." She took a shaky breath. "This is partly my fault. I promise you, I'll do everything in my power to make things right again."

Gary stared at her, confused. "Is this about Eden?"

Hope surged inside Brianna. "Did you see her?"

Malik glanced over, his face brightening slightly.

Gary shook his head. "No. But Lois was acting kinda strange yesterday."

Air whooshed out of Brianna.

"Eden's missing," she confessed in a deflated voice. "She ran away from home last night."

Gary's eyes widened. "Oh God! I'm so sorry, Brianna!"

"Don't be." A sad smile twisted Brianna's lips. "I'm to blame for that too."

Gary gazed at his home as he was lifted into the back of the last ambulance.

"Do you know what attacked us?" he murmured. "It happened so quickly I couldn't tell. The only thing I remember is that awful smell."

Brianna stiffened, alarmed. "A smell?"

Malik came over, his expression mirroring her sudden tension.

"What kind of smell?" Brianna asked Gary urgently.

"It was like something dead." He wrinkled his nose. "Like meat gone bad."

Malik swore. Brianna scowled, her hands fisting at her sides.

Ghouls!

Gary stared at them. "Do you know who they were?"

"We have an inkling," Brianna replied in a steely voice. She turned to Malik. "Divert the ambulances to the magic ward at San Francisco Memorial. If ghouls attacked them, their wounds will reopen again. They need Blossom Silver and Glitterfang to cure them."

The ambulance door closed on Gary's stunned face.

Remorse shot through Brianna as she watched the vehicle drive off. She'd always hoped to keep the Serranos away from the world of magic. Unfortunately, their encounter with ghouls meant they were about to receive a fast-track introduction into that troublesome world. A grim smile tugged at her mouth despite the graveness of the situation.

She suspected Lois knew half of it already.

Brianna went over to join Malik where he was giving rapid instructions to the team of Hexa agents on site. She knew she would have to have him call this in to Argonaut shortly. This incident fell squarely within the agency's remit.

Hexa would need to be involved by virtue of the Serranos' association with Eden and San Francisco PD were bound to have a say in the matter too, since the Serranos were non-magic-users. Still, with ghouls involved, Argonaut would take the lead on this investigation. She narrowed her eyes.

Luckily, Francis still owes me for what happened with Chester Moran and those sorcerers. I'll have to convince him to keep Eden's disappearance under wraps for now.

Trepidation throbbed through Brianna. Ghouls were blood-drinking and flesh-eating monsters who normally dwelled in the Shadow Empire. Though their presence had been sighted in the human world on many an occasion in the past few hundred years, it was rare for them to venture into a city.

She knew they had to be after Eden. As for the reason why, she hoped and prayed she would find out before they got to her daughter.

Please be safe, wherever you are!

CHAPTER TWELVE

"Lightning Flash," Maggie Briggs said confidently.

Bailey looked blank. "Come again?"

The witch pushed her glasses up the bridge of her nose. "Hmm. I guess it's not something you guys would have heard of before. I only learned about it at magic university myself."

Cassius narrowed his eyes. The term was vaguely familiar.

"Lightning Flash is a mineral mined from the mountains around the Astrea Sea," Maggie explained. "In its dormant state, it can be used to combat Demon Rot, a flesh-eating disease originating from the Hells that plagued Europe and Asia during the late eighteenth, early nineteenth centuries. Mixed with electrum and gunpowder, it becomes a powerful explosive with a small radius of focus. Ideal if you want to destroy something big without making too much of a bang. Like a bank vault door."

"Hmm," Lucy Walters murmured. "That sounds dangerous."

The Argonaut chief medical mage poured sugar into her coffee and stirred it with magic before taking a sip.

Lambert and Willis looked at her warily. The two detectives had come to the agency bureau to find out the results of Maggie's analysis.

Morgan grunted. "Is there a reason why you're here?"

Lucy indicated her sandwich, expression innocent. "I'm on my lunch break."

"There's a perfectly satisfactory break room on the top floor of this building," Morgan pointed out. "Why aren't you there?"

"Don't be such a party pooper. I'm keeping Maggie company." A saccharine smile stretched her mouth as she glanced between Morgan and Cassius. "By the way, Cassius is glowing like a bride freshly back from her honeymoon. You two must have been busy."

Cassius's ears grew warm. It took all his effort not to touch his face.

Morgan scowled.

"Oh. You guys are..." Lambert trailed off, her curious gaze swinging between the two angels.

Willis's eyes rounded slightly.

"What I do with Cassius is no one's business but ours," Morgan growled at Lucy.

Cassius bit back a sigh. Morgan's possessiveness was cute but damn awkward at times.

The Aerial turned to Maggie. "This Lightning Flash, is it freely available on the market?"

Maggie shook her head. "Like I said, I've only come across it in books. It hasn't been seen or heard of since Demon Rot was eradicated. Argonaut keeps samples of every magic substance ever discovered, hence why I was able to crossmatch its profile."

"So, you were right," Lambert told Morgan with a frown. "These assholes really were trying not to draw attention to themselves."

Cassius drummed a hand on his knee. They'd visited all nine crime scenes yesterday and had discovered faint traces of enchantment magic at every one of them. The only Altered Mind box they'd found thus far was at the first bank they'd gone to in the morning. The item was currently being examined by Charlie and the Argonaut tech department.

"We should contact our informants," Adrianne told Morgan. "Ask them if they've heard of a recent trade in Lightning Flash."

"We'll do the same," Willis muttered. "They wouldn't normally know about magic and stuff, but there's no harm asking them."

Morgan dipped his chin. "Do that."

"There's someone we know who's had something to do with the Astrea Sea recently," Zach pondered.

"Ah." Julia brightened. "Our alchemist."

"What alchemist?" Lambert said blankly.

"Oh, just a guy who helped bag me a table at *Revelations*," the angel said dismissively.

Willis raised his eyebrows, impressed. "That new Michelin-starred restaurant on North Beach?"

Lambert stared at the detective.

The older man shrugged. "I was thinking of taking the wife there for our anniversary."

"I'll put a word in for you with the owner," Julia said graciously.

"Adrianne and Bailey, you take the alchemist," Morgan instructed. "The rest of us will return to the crime scenes with Lambert and Willis. We still haven't figured out how the robbers got in and out of those banks."

"We should contact Hexa and the other agencies," Cassius suggested as they started for the exit. "They might know of magic or otherwordly artifacts being kept in a bank vault in San Francisco."

Morgan nodded.

They bumped into Zakir Singh in the underground garage. The Argonaut agent had initially been hostile when Cassius had been arrested and brought to the bureau a month ago, as had most of the agency's staff. Cassius's battles alongside Morgan and his team against Chester Moran and his black-magic sorcerers had soon changed their minds. Many of those who'd been present at the incident on Nob Hill owed their lives to the two angels.

"You guys look busy," Julia remarked as they headed for their respective vehicles.

Cassius stared, curious. A couple of medical mages were accompanying Singh's team.

"Hexa reported an attack on non-magic-users at a

private residence in Presidio Heights this morning," Singh said. "We're on our way to check it out."

Zach arched an eyebrow. "Since when do we get involved in non-magic-user incidents?"

Lambert and Willis looked over at Singh, equally puzzled.

Singh made a face. "Hexa seems to think ghouls were involved."

Surprise shot through Cassius. "Ghouls?"

"Yeah. One of the witnesses reported a smell of rotting meat at the time of the attack."

Cassius was still pondering Singh's words as he and Morgan drove out of the garage. It was exceedingly rare to see ghouls about these days and they weren't the kind of creatures who would venture into the city.

I wonder what that's about.

They'd decided to split into three teams of two to cover more ground. Morgan and Cassius had just finished examining the neighborhood surrounding the eighth bank that had been targeted by the robbers and were on their way to the last crime scene when Adrianne rang.

"Our alchemist gave us something in exchange for a plea bargain. He said there was a rumor circulating about a secret and exceedingly valuable shipment that came in from the Astrea Sea a couple of months back. He didn't know what it was but the dealer who apparently handled the sale is someone reputed to work with rare and banned substances. Guy's name is Usman Abbas."

"Did he come up on our database?" Morgan asked with a frown.

He'd put his cell on speaker so Cassius could hear the conversation.

"Yeah. This guy's criminal record is a mile long. He's on San Francisco PD's radar too. His whereabouts are currently unknown, so we'll have to go hunting if we want to find him."

"You and Bailey do that," Morgan said. "We'll keep investigating the crime scenes."

"Will do." Adrianne paused. "Anything come up at your end yet?"

Morgan sighed. "No."

He ended the call just as a tram trundled past them. They were halfway across the road when he slowed and stopped. Cassius looked at him, puzzled.

Morgan was staring at the light-rail train where it had stopped at a station. Honks sounded around them, the traffic jerking to a halt to avoid running them over.

"Er, Morgan? We should move."

"The subway." Morgan's gaze swung stiffly to Cassius. "No one thought to check the subway!"

CHAPTER THIRTEEN

EDEN PUT HER TOILETRIES INSIDE HER VANITY BAG AND headed out of the bathroom facilities at the youth hostel in Mission Dolores. It was early afternoon and she'd just settled into the room she'd be sharing with three other people for the next two nights.

She'd taken care to choose a cheap place somewhere far from any neighborhoods that might be being monitored by Hexa in one way or another. The hostel receptionist who'd booked her in hadn't batted an eyelid when Eden had shown her her fake ID. Even if Brianna and Hexa scoured the internet for any digital trace of her presence, they wouldn't find it. As for putting in a missing person report with the local police, Eden doubted her mother would go that far.

It was in Hexa and Brianna's interest to keep her disappearance a secret.

She quelled her melancholic thoughts, packed her things inside the secure locker she'd been assigned, and went in search of a cyber cafe. She found one half a mile from the hostel and bought a coach ticket to San Diego. Since she'd ditched her cellphone and had yet to buy a new one, she sent an email to the farm she'd secured a position at to let them know she would be arriving in a couple of days. She spent the next few hours scouring the internet for colleges close to the place. Even though she'd bought a fake high school diploma, she still intended to complete her studies.

It was dark by the time Eden logged out of the public computer. She shivered when she stepped out of the cafe. A chilly wind was blowing across the city from the bay, heralding the change of seasons. San Diego in autumn would be warmer than San Francisco. She hunched her shoulders and zipped up her parka.

I should buy some food before I go back.

She got Chinese takeout at a small restaurant close by and decided to eat it while she headed for the hostel. A strange feeling settled over her as she strolled along the half-empty streets, her steps light. It took a while for her to figure out what it was.

Freedom.

She had never felt as relaxed and carefree as she did in this moment. It was as if a giant weight had finally been lifted off her shoulders.

For the first time in years, Eden experienced a surge of optimism.

Getting away from my mother and Hexa was the right thing to do.

She'd almost finished her food and was wondering what to do the next day when a sudden stillness descended around her. Eden slowed and stopped, her skin prickling.

She'd cut across a narrow lane running past a cemetery and church, a shortcut to the hostel. She looked over her shoulder, unease quickening her pulse.

The path behind her was deserted.

Eden stared into the shadows for breathless moments before turning to resume her route. Something shifted in the gloom some hundred feet ahead of her. She froze.

A figure was blocking the lane exit. Another stepped into view next to it. A stench wafted toward Eden. Her eyes widened.

It was the smell of rotting meat.

The guttural rasp that reached her next had her belly clenching in terror. It was a hungry sound. One that craved mayhem and death.

Eden knew instinctively that she was in mortal danger. Yet, her limbs refused to budge.

Move! MOVE, dammit!

The figures lunged toward her.

She twisted on her heels, her body finally unfreezing, the carton of cooling food dropping from her grasp and spilling onto the ground. She staggered to an abrupt halt in the next instant, her breath locking painfully in her throat. Two more shapes were racing along the ground toward her from the opposite end of the lane.

They were not human.

Eden whirled around and jumped onto the fence to her right. She scaled it in a flash, climbed over, and landed awkwardly in the grounds of the cemetery, cuts blooming on her hands from the barbed wire.

The night closed in around her as she darted between trees and bushes, the gravestones looming out of the shadows silent witnesses to the chase. She didn't have to look behind her to know her pursuers were hot on her trail. She could smell their foul breath on her heels and sense their murderous gaze on her back.

She emerged into an open area next to a water fountain and saw a faint light in one of the rear windows of the chapel that abutted the church. Her heart thumped with a wild burst of hope.

"Help!" Eden shouted. "Please, help—!"

She tripped and fell, her words choking off to a gasp. Air whooshed out of her as she hit the ground hard. Her head struck the courtyard paving. Stars exploded across her vision.

Eden lay stunned for a moment, the world swimming dizzyingly around her.

Get up!

She gritted her teeth and crawled onto her hands and knees, sticky wetness trickling down her forehead from the gash in her hairline. Growls sounded behind her, hot and ravenous.

Eden fumbled for the knife in her pocket, her fingers made clumsy by panic. She staggered to her feet and turned, knuckles white on the handle of the blade, knowing she would have to make her final stand here.

The monsters loomed out of the shadows, their grotesque shapes finally taking form under the starlight. A whimper tumbled from Eden's lips, unbidden.

The creatures were six feet tall and all muscle and sinew, their skin stretched tightly over their misshapen bones and their flesh oozing with weeping sores. Their crimson eyes shone brightly as they gazed upon her, drool falling in thick flecks from long, wicked fangs.

Nausea twisted Eden's stomach at the vile miasma emanating from them.

The one who appeared to be the leader of the group grunted at its companions and gestured at them with its head. The other three fanned out around her, low growls rumbling from their throats.

Eden blinked blood out of her eye and swallowed, confusion overriding her terror for a moment. She'd expected to be dead by now.

Why aren't they attacking?!

The leader reached a clawed hand toward her. Eden gasped and stumbled back, her arm swinging up automatically.

Her knife caught the monster's little finger and sliced it in half.

Bile flooded her throat. She gagged and brought a hand to her mouth, her grip loosening on the blade, her legs shaking.

The monster glared at her and leapt, its roar echoing in her ears.

Brightness punctured the gloom.

A blazing sphere of emerald light smashed into the creature's flank as it soared toward her. The monster went flying into a gravestone, flesh and bone giving way with a wet crunch. Its companions whirled around, snarls rising in the night as they glowered at the figure approaching rapidly from the right.

Eden's heart stuttered.

It was the guy from the restaurant two days ago. The one who'd captured her attention and that of every other girl in the place.

"You idiot, what are you doing?!" the stranger barked.

CHAPTER FOURTEEN

Cedric Esteban glared at the young girl standing frozen amidst the ghouls. It had taken him the whole day to track her down after getting rid of the monsters who'd been after her in the park by the beach last night.

And here she is again, in the middle of yet another shitshow!

"Par—pardon?!" the girl stammered, shocked.

Cedric sent a silent prayer to the ancient Dryad Gods. *Save me from human fools!*

"I said, what the hell are you doing? Get away from here!"

Magic swelled inside him as he bolted across the cemetery, the laurel staff in his grasp channeling the otherworldly power in his soul core. Incandescent light exploded in his left hand, the green glow washing over the graveyard. He cast the explosive spell bomb at the ghoul closest to the girl.

She cried out in shock as the monster went sailing through the air and smashed into the water fountain.

Cedric dropped and slid between the remaining two ghouls. They moved to rip his flesh from his bones, their claws glinting as their arms descended toward him. They grunted when the staff smashed into their legs, taking them to the ground.

Cedric knew their surprise would only last a moment.

I need to get us out of here, now!

He rolled, leapt to his feet, and grabbed the startled girl's hand. A choked sound left her as he pelted for the side of the building looming next to them, dragging her forcefully along. The ghouls were already rising, a flicker out the corner of his eye.

"What—what's going on here?!" someone gasped behind them.

Cedric skidded to a stop and whirled around, the girl slipping and almost falling beside him. A man in a black cassock had come out of the chapel's back door. His gaze swung to them before locking on the monsters. Incomprehension widened his eyes.

Shit!

"Get back inside!" Cedric shouted.

He couldn't afford to stop and assist the priest. Not if he wanted to get them far away enough to avoid the ghouls' detection. The creatures' ability to sniff out their prey's scent was legendary in the realms.

"Please," the girl mumbled. "We need to help him!"

Cedric glanced at her. She met his gaze squarely,

her own full of despair and equal determination. He hesitated before drawing on his magic.

A ghoul leapt onto the frozen priest before he could cast the spell bomb. The girl whimpered as the man's cry rent the air, the sound turning to a wet gurgle when the ghoul ripped open his throat.

Cedric cursed and started running.

There was no helping the priest now.

The girl stumbled as they turned the corner, her fingers clenching tightly around his. Heat shot up his arm, startling him. The blackthorn and alder bracelet on his wrist trembled. Before he could fathom what was happening, they found themselves in a narrow courtyard.

Cedric's pulse raced as he frantically scanned the area for an escape route.

The girl pointed at a gap in the shadows to their right. "There!"

It was a path barely three feet wide that cut between the chapel and the main church building.

It'll have to do!

He darted swiftly toward it, the girl keeping pace.

Tiles smashed and clattered above them as the ghouls took to the roof. Shadows danced over their heads. Cedric glanced up, his heart thundering against his ribs.

Two of the creatures had cleared the gap between the buildings. Their claws scrabbled frantically for purchase on the opposite wall. They leapt and bounded along the vertical rise, chunks of plaster crumbling beneath their fierce grip, their motion defying gravity as they kept level with Cedric and the girl.

A narrow, gated wall loomed up ahead, beyond another small courtyard. Cedric clenched his jaw.

The ghouls would attack them there.

"Stay behind me!" he yelled at the girl.

They emerged inside the enclosed space. The ghouls dropped down on them with vicious snarls, dark shapes against the starlit night.

Cedric spun the laurel staff and blocked their attacks, the wood humming and vibrating violently as he smashed the weapon into the monsters' heads and bodies, his movements swift and sure. He cast magic spell bombs at them before they could recover, hoping to stun them for the precious seconds he and the girl would need to climb over the wall.

Alarm twisted his gut. His eyes widened.

Wait! There's only three of them! Where the hell is the—?!

A gasp reached him from behind. He looked over his shoulder.

The fourth ghoul had sneaked around the rooftop of the chapel and was descending the wall toward the girl. She stumbled back a couple of steps, fear leeching the color from her face.

Claws glinted at the edge of Cedric's vision. He leaned sharply at the waist and narrowly missed the monster's attempt to gouge his eye out. The staff sang in his hands as he spun low on his feet. He rose and jabbed the sharp end into the throat of the creature.

The ghoul gurgled, blood spurting from the deadly wound and dripping down the wood.

Heat bloomed on Cedric's left arm. He backfisted the ghoul who'd ripped his skin open in the face, kicked the one lunging at him in the gut, and yanked his staff out of the dying monster. He whirled around in time to see the fourth ghoul slash the girl across the belly with a wicked claw.

She gasped, one hand rising to clutch the crimson stain blossoming on her clothes, the other loosening around the handle of her knife. The weapon fell from her limp fingers and clattered to the ground, the sound loud in Cedric's ears.

"*No!*"

He moved, fury sending blood roaring in his veins.

The ghoul turned its head and glared at him. It was the leader of the group.

The monster blocked Cedric's staff with a raised arm and punched him in the chest. Cedric grunted as he went sailing backward. He smashed into the wall a couple of feet to the girl's right, plaster cracking beneath him. Pain squeezed his ribs, robbing him of breath. He winced, the disquiet dancing at the back of his mind growing ten-fold.

These creatures! They're not normal!

The ghoul focused on its prey once more, its intent all too clear. The girl met Cedric's gaze as the monster prepared to spring, her pupils reflecting his horror. He raged at his body to move.

His limbs refused to obey his commands.

She stretched out a hand toward him. "Run!"

Cedric lifted an arm toward her, his body heavy and his heart clenching with an agony he couldn't explain. Blood flicked from her fingers and landed on his face and wrist. A drop splattered onto the blackthorn and alder bracelet.

A powerful echo resonated from the wooden bangle. Cedric froze.

The world held its breath.

Crimson incandescence detonated around his wrist, silent and powerful, the acrid scent of magic following it.

Though he knew what followed was but a phenomenon born of the adrenaline filling his blood, Cedric couldn't help but stare in awe as time seemed to slow, everything around him growing sluggish, as if they were moving on the bottom of a deep ocean.

The bracelet trembled and grew hot, warming his skin yet somehow not burning it. Cedric's stunned gaze locked on the shimmering wood and the hidden artifact slowly emerging from the powerful spell that had concealed it.

It was a small, wooden pendant shaped like a tree.

Light drew his gaze. His pulse stuttered.

The girl's wound was shining with the same scarlet glow, the radiance emerging from somewhere deep inside her. Understanding dawned, making him blink.

Dread formed a leaden pit in the bottom of Cedric's stomach.

Her soul core. It's bloodcursed! But—how?!

He hadn't been able to fathom why he'd felt the inane urge to follow the girl since he first laid eyes on her in that restaurant, two days ago. He'd sensed the ghouls shadowing her that afternoon and had been curious as to why the monsters were after her. He hadn't realized it was the artifact he had been sent to Earth to protect that had resonated with her from the moment of their meeting and had sought to get close to her since.

The girl's head moved, her startled gaze dropping to her belly and the unholy light pulsing from her body. Red lines darted across her skin like cracks on parched earth, the blaze spreading even as her wound closed.

The ghoul leapt, powerful legs lifting off the ground, its body stretching languidly in a deadly arc.

The girl gasped. Her head snapped back and her spine grew rigid, the muscles and tendons in her neck and limbs straining to the point Cedric feared they would tear. Her hair rose, fanning out in a halo around her, red static dancing on the blonde tips. Her slender frame levitated a few inches into the air.

The inhuman scream that tore from her throat made Cedric's eardrums throb.

Power exploded from within the girl, so violent it drenched the air with a scarlet haze and sent fracture lines dancing across the ground and up the walls of the chapel and the church. Her arm moved, her hand opening wide as she raised it toward the ghoul dropping toward her in slow motion, her brow furrowed in an expression of pure wrath. A red sphere burst into existence on her palm.

Her magic tore a hole straight through the ghoul's

chest, blasted a crater into the chapel wall behind it, and took out a section of the roof.

The flow of time resumed with a rush of cool air and the stench of burnt flesh, the monster's dying screech echoing in the night. Debris rained down into the courtyard, fragments of wood, tiles, and plaster clouding the air.

A ghoul came at the girl from the left. She flicked her hand.

The monster went flying toward the roof of the chapel, its guttural cry cut off abruptly when its neck broke.

Cedric rose and blocked the last ghoul's strike with his laurel staff before it could land on the girl. The monster roared and lunged at him, all fangs and claws and crimson eyes. Its head imploded in the next instant, the destructive magic the girl had cast crushing its skull and brain to mush. The ghoul crumpled to the ground, limbs twitching and jerking briefly before it grew still. Cedric swallowed bile and wiped the creature's blood from his face with the back of his hand, his heart pounding.

Deafening silence descended on the courtyard.

The girl swayed, the crimson lines that had lit her flesh fading as rapidly as they had formed, the glow in the middle of her body subsiding.

"What," she mumbled, "what just—?!"

Her eyes rolled back in her head.

Cedric caught her before she hit the ground. She felt light in his arms, much lighter than he'd thought she would be. And cold. He stared at her ashen face for a long moment before lifting her effortlessly onto his shoulder, the ramifications of what had unfolded here tonight making his belly clench with unease.

He would have to let the Dryad kingdom know of this development.

Cedric kicked down the gate and marched out into the night with his unconscious charge, the smell of death fading behind him.

CHAPTER FIFTEEN

"SHIT."

Lambert shone her flashlight at the dark opening above them, a scowl on her face.

"So, this is how these bastards got in?" Willis said bitterly.

"Seems that way," Morgan muttered.

His gut instinct about the subway had been correct. After exploring the underground station next to the last crime scene, he and Cassius had found a hidden opening along the tracks. The mage magic concealing it had been muted by a powerful spell, making it practically undetectable. It was only thanks to Cassius's sensitive nose that they'd uncovered the juniper scent that had lingered on the fake metal partition.

The tunnel they'd discovered beyond it had ended in a bore hole carved vertically into the floor of one of the bank's boiler rooms. The opening at the other end had been similarly camouflaged under a concrete paving supported by metal poles and a concealment spell.

Once they'd known what to look for, Morgan's team had uncovered an identical setup at all the crime scenes, including the one they were currently at near the Civic Center.

Morgan's unease had deepened throughout the afternoon and evening. The care taken in committing these infractions was on a whole other level. It was evident the schemes the perpetrators had put in place had been a long time in the making. Yet, their motive remained elusive, a fact he found troubling.

He'd had Julia and Zach liaise with the city's Transportation Agency to release the camera recordings of the subway tunnels where the hidden openings had been found. His instincts told him the perpetrators would have taken care of those videos too, but there was no harm asking. Cassius had agreed.

As for Adrianne and Bailey, they still hadn't found any clues as to Usman Abbas's whereabouts. Charlie was still stuck in the lab at the bureau analyzing the Altered Mind box. Morgan frowned.

Looks like we're just going to have to cool our heels until we get a fresh lead.

He and Cassius exited the tunnel ahead of Lambert and Willis. They had just turned to make their way back to the subway station when Cassius stopped.

The angel looked over his shoulder. A faint frown furrowed his brow.

Morgan tensed. He knew that look. "What is it?"

"I'm…not sure." Cassius twisted around and took a

few steps past the hidden tunnel opening. "There's a scent of something."

He stiffened a moment later.

Morgan's pulse quickened at Cassius's expression. Whatever he'd just detected, it was bad.

"Can you make your way back to the station?" He glanced at the two detectives, his expression wary. "Cassius and I need to stay down here a bit longer."

Lambert and Willis exchanged a puzzled look.

"Sure," Lambert murmured. "Does this have anything to do with the robberies?"

"I'm not certain," Cassius replied in Morgan's stead. "It's too dangerous for you to follow us in these tunnels."

The detectives nodded reluctantly and headed back.

Morgan waited until their steps had faded before gazing somberly at Cassius. "What's wrong?"

"I can smell ghouls," Cassius said grimly.

Alarm shot through Morgan. His gaze swung to the maw of darkness ahead of them. "Are they close?"

Cassius shook his head. "No. The scent is fresh but far. We need to find out where it's coming from."

Morgan headed wordlessly into the gloom after Cassius.

The presence of ghouls in the city would spread fear if it became widely known. The creatures were renowned not only for their thirst for human flesh, but for being deadly hunters. If a pack of those monsters had somehow made its way into San Francisco, Argonaut would have to move fast to neutralize them before they could hurt anyone. He frowned.

Judging from the attack Zakir and his team were sent to investigate, it might already be too late for that.

They navigated the subway system in silence, keeping to the safety areas and walkways when they detected approaching trains. With their preternatural sight and hearing, being down there didn't pose a danger to them. Even if they were to be accidentally struck by a train, they were unlikely to perish, their bodies strong enough to smash through metal.

They emerged somewhere close to the 16th Street Mission station, Cassius following a trail that led them into the sewer adjoining the subway and up a ladder to a rusted manhole that opened into the yard of a derelict warehouse one street over.

A cool breeze blew in from the bay and ruffled their hair as they headed west. The wind changed direction a moment later. Morgan slowed, tension swirling through him.

He could smell the stench of rotting meat Cassius had detected in the subway.

They picked up pace and headed for a bell tower looming against the night sky farther down the road. Cassius pressed a hand to Morgan's chest when they reached the corner of the intersection, halting him in his tracks.

They stared at the dark buildings of a church and a chapel on the opposite side of the road.

Even Morgan could feel the eerie magic tainting the air.

"Be careful," Cassius warned. "Whoever this is, their magic is powerful."

"Do you know what it is?" Morgan asked in a low voice as they crossed the road. "I've never felt anything like it."

"I have my suspicions." Cassius frowned. "I've only sensed something like this once before. It didn't end well for anyone."

Their footsteps led them to a narrow passage between the church and the chapel. The alley ended in a gated wall. The wooden door had been smashed open and lay in pieces on the ground.

Cassius and Morgan reached for their daggers as they approached the opening, senses on high alert.

CHAPTER SIXTEEN

"Hurry!" Brianna gasped.

Malik clenched his teeth and floored the pedal. The SUV jerked forward, the seat belt digging painfully into Brianna's chest.

They were well over the speed limit and had been so for the past one and a half miles.

Brianna's heart raced and her breathing came fast and shallow. She clutched her stomach and bit back another moan, sweat beading her forehead. Though the agonizing pain had subsided, spasms still gripped her occasionally.

She had been at the office when it had started, too stressed about Eden's disappearance to go home. The Hexa agents who had scoured the city for signs of her daughter all day hadn't reported any sightings of her as of yet, much to Brianna's frustration.

She could feel time running out for both her and Eden.

Brianna had just gotten up from her desk to get a

glass of water when searing heat had blossomed inside her body, robbing her of breath. Malik had detected the burst of magic that had rippled outward from her soul core and had rushed inside the office, only to find her on her knees, face drained of blood and teeth biting down hard on her lip to muffle the scream threatening to burst from her.

Brianna had known instinctively that Eden's bloodcursed magic had awakened. This was the same pain she used to endure when Eden was just a child and her spellbound soul core wildly unstable. Except this agony was ten times, no, twenty times worse.

As impossible as it seemed, something had broken through the powerful conjurations keeping her daughter's magic at bay.

Brianna had refused to let a Hexa medical mage look her over and had insisted Malik get her to a vehicle and drive across the city. She could feel an echo of Eden's powers coming from the southwest. Though it wasn't the way she'd hoped to find her daughter, the accursed link between them meant Brianna had some sort of way of tracking Eden's magic now that it was free.

They took a sharp left at an intersection and were soon in Mission Dolores.

Brianna closed her eyes briefly, nausea roiling through her. The closer she got to what was drawing her, the more she sensed her daughter's pain and fear.

Eden! Please be safe, baby!

"Take the next right!" she ordered seconds later.

Malik obeyed her command wordlessly.

The sorcerer knew what was going on. As the one in charge of Eden's bodyguards, he had once witnessed an episode where Eden's bloodcursed magic had resonated with Brianna, when Eden was four. Brianna had had little choice but to reveal the circumstances behind the incident and swear the sorcerer to secrecy. In all the time since then, Malik had never revealed what he knew to any of his team members or Hexa, his fierce loyalty and devotion to her and Eden something Brianna was eternally grateful for. Brianna knew Malik hated that he and the Hexa agents in charge of guarding her daughter were not supposed to get too physically close to her because of her cursed magic.

A church appeared on the road they were navigating. Brianna had Malik stop next to it. She climbed unsteadily out of the SUV. The bloodcursed taint lingering in the air made her chest tighten with alarm, the pungent smell stinging her nostrils. Malik put an arm around her waist to support her as they headed down the sidewalk and followed the residue of uncanny magic dancing in the wind. But it wasn't Eden they found when they turned the corner into a narrow passageway between the church and the chapel.

Cassius Black and Morgan King were crouched in the middle of a narrow courtyard beyond the smashed gate at the end of the path. The two angels stiffened when they detected their presence and rose swiftly to their feet, their hands going for their guns. They froze and relaxed when they recognized Brianna, surprise flaring across their faces.

"Brianna?" Cassius said.

Brianna's gaze shifted to the remains of the monster Cassius and Morgan had been examining. Icy fingers clutched her heart. Malik glanced at her, anxious.

Morgan frowned. "What are you doing here?"

"My daughter," Brianna said in a low voice. "Is she here?"

She didn't dare look at the bodies she could see on the ground behind the two angels. Cassius and Morgan shared a startled look.

"No," Cassius replied. "The only human we found was a priest, in the cemetery on the other side of the chapel." Concern clouded his face as he gazed at her. "What's going on, Brianna? You look—"

"Pretty damn awful," Morgan muttered.

Brianna sagged against Malik, the breath she'd been holding whooshing out of her.

"Thank God!" she mumbled. "I thought—I really thought—!"

She paused and swallowed convulsively, her vision blurring with tears. Malik's fingers sank into her flank where he held her, his concern palpable.

"Were these ghouls after your daughter?" Cassius asked, his tone firm but kind.

Brianna nodded shakily. "Yes. I believe so."

She couldn't hide the truth any longer.

Morgan's gaze switched between Brianna and Malik. "The attack Hexa reported to Argonaut earlier today. Did that involve your daughter too?"

Brianna inhaled raggedly before dipping her chin.

The sound of rapidly approaching vehicles rose from the street next to the church. Two Argonaut

SUVs screeched to a stop at the curb. The rest of Morgan's team bar the enchanter spilled out onto the sidewalk and approached at a jog.

"Any survivors?" Adrianne called out.

Cassius shook his head, chagrined. "No. The priest is long dead. There was no one else in the place, which is something to be thankful for, I guess. The ghouls wouldn't have let them live, for sure."

Julia and Zach stared at the jagged crater in the wall of the chapel. They could see clear through to the inside of the building and the hole in the roof.

"What the hell happened here?" Bailey said leadenly.

Morgan narrowed his eyes at Brianna and Malik. "That's what we'd like to know."

Brianna straightened, Malik reluctantly letting her go.

Though her heart was heavy and dread still ate at her insides, she would have to confess to her crimes if there was to be any chance of saving her daughter. Something told her the two angels facing her were likely the only ones who could do that.

The day of reckoning for my past deeds has finally come.

"It would be best if we talked about this back at Argonaut," she told Morgan and Cassius in a lifeless voice.

CHAPTER SEVENTEEN

Pain throbbed through Eden's temples when she came to. She moaned and stirred, plastic crinkling beneath her as she shifted on a springy surface. She blinked, her throat parched and her belly clenching on a wave of hunger.

A moldy ceiling swam into view above her, water stains marking the concrete in cloud-like patterns.

"Here."

Eden startled and twisted her head around.

The headache stabbed at her skull, a hammer drill that made her eyes throb with black spots. She bit her lip to stop the moan rising from her throat. Her vision cleared.

The guy who'd saved her from the monsters was waving a can of soda and a chocolate bar at her from where he sat on a pile of breeze blocks.

Memory returned in a flood of gruesome images and sounds.

Eden gasped and sat up, her heart lurching.

She was lying on a tarpaulin-covered mattress. She clutched at her stomach, her wild gaze seeking the wound the creature had slashed into her flesh. Her pulse stuttered.

It was gone.

Her bare skin was free from blemish where it peeked through the gash in her clothes.

"What—how?!" she mumbled. Her gaze found his left arm. "Your wound! Is it—?"

"My wound is fine. I put some ointment on it." The guy sighed. "Eat and drink first. Your head must be hurting from the lack of sugar."

Eden realized he was right. She was famished. She hesitated before taking the chocolate bar and soda. She examined the items warily.

"They're not poisoned." He flashed a grim smile. "If I'd wanted you dead, I would have left you to those monsters."

Eden popped open the soda and unwrapped the chocolate bar. Her stomach grumbled loudly at their sweet scents. She flushed, conscious of the guy's unwavering stare. Amusement danced in his eyes as he watched her wolf them down. Eden's face grew warm. She looked around as she swallowed the last mouthful of chocolate, as much to escape his piercing gaze as to figure out their whereabouts.

They were on the second floor of an abandoned warehouse. She could see lights on a distant shoreline through a broken window to her left and smell the sea on the breeze rattling the plastic sheets covering some of the empty frames.

"Where are we?" Eden said.

"Somewhere safe, for now," he replied, his expression growing guarded. "My name is Cedric. What's yours?"

She hesitated. "Eden."

"Ah." A mocking expression danced across his handsome face. "The Garden of God."

Eden narrowed her eyes slightly. She was beginning to realize that Cedric was a bit of a jerk, despite his good looks. Not to mention his fighting skills. He could easily match Malik in a magic duel.

She put the empty can of soda on the ground beside the mattress, her mind abuzz with questions. If anyone knew the answers to them, it was bound to be Cedric. She wasn't sure where to begin.

His next words stole the wind from her sails.

"How have you been able to survive so long with a bloodcursed soul core?"

Eden stared at him, nonplussed. "What?"

"Your soul core. You have bloodcursed magic flowing through it." He frowned at her stunned expression. "You didn't know?"

"You must be mistaken." Eden swallowed in the silence. "I don't possess any magic."

"I beg to differ," Cedric retorted coolly. "You didn't kill those ghouls back there with your pretty words. That was magic and bloodcursed magic at that."

The incident at the church danced through Eden's mind as if it were a dream. She remembered the monster cutting her with his claws. And she recalled the rage and anguish in Cedric's eyes as he tried to come to her aid but was unable to. What had happened next was a series of chaotic snapshots that didn't seem real.

The red light that had burst into life on Cedric's bracelet. The fire that had flooded her blood and flesh in reaction to it. The insane power that had risen from deep inside her in a violent tide that had threatened to swallow her whole. The wrath that had filled her veins and brought forth a sphere of explosive, crimson energy which had pulverized the body of the monster who had been lunging at her.

Those were ghouls?!

She'd read about the creatures in one of her books. They were evil spirits who dwelled in the Nine Hells and were avid consumers of human flesh. They were famed for carrying a stench of rotting meat.

Eden blinked, startled.

That day outside the restaurant. They were the ones following me!

"But I—I was born magicless!" she protested numbly.

Cedric frowned. "Who told you that?"

"My mother." Eden faltered. "And Hexa."

"Well, they lied." Cedric grunted. "You have magic, alright. Powerful, cursed magic."

It was a moment before Eden could speak.

"Why—?" She stopped and swallowed, confusion swirling through her, muddling her mind. "Why would they do such a thing? Lie, I mean?"

Cedric sighed, frown fading and expression growing tired.

"Because bloodcursed magic is damned. It's a devastating kind of magic. The scant humans who have been ill-fated enough to be born with it in the last few hundred years have all met dire fates. By that, I mean they're dead."

Eden felt light-headed.

"They pretty much self-destructed," Cedric continued, heedless of her shock. "Human souls just aren't strong enough to hold that amount of magic. Most bloodcursed magic users never make it past their tenth birthday. In fact, the only way someone with bloodcursed magic could theoretically survive to adulthood would be if—"

He stopped abruptly, his eyes widening.

"If what?" Eden croaked.

She couldn't believe what she was hearing. That she somehow possessed magic and had done so all along. Though she didn't want to accept what Cedric was saying, she knew the words he'd spoken were the truth. There was no other explanation for what had happened back at that church.

Besides, she could feel it in the marrow of her bones and in the warm spot behind her belly button. The place where she could sense something she had never felt before.

Power.

Despite his brusque tone and sarcastic manner, Cedric's eyes shone with an honesty and frankness she rarely encountered in her day-to-day life. He had no reason to lie to her.

"If what?" Eden repeated as he stared blindly at her, his face pale.

"If their soul core was bound from birth." His words fell heavily between them. "If a human with bloodcursed magic were to have their soul confined when they were born, then they might technically be saved from their fate. But that kind of spell is exceedingly difficult to pull off. You would need several high-powered magic users to do it. And that wouldn't be the end of the story. The spellbound soul core would likely be unstable and would need to be carefully monitored. The likelihood of sudden flare-ups would be high, and these would engender immense suffering in both the one possessing the bloodcursed soul core and the magic user who would need to temper it."

An image of her mother rose before Eden's eyes as Cedric's words sank into her consciousness. She had a vague memory of seeing Brianna in pain when she was a very young child. She could dimly recall her own whimpers as she'd lain on the ground, a relentless pressure building inside her small body moments before the world went dark around her.

She had always thought it a nightmare.

Malik was there too, I think.

Eden stared at her hands, her heart pounding. She slowly flexed her fingers, as if seeing them for the first time. Anger swelled inside her, along with regret and a sorrow so deep it almost brought her to tears.

Is that what this has all been about? Brianna acting the

way she has all these years and Hexa guarding me day and night? Is it because of my bloodcursed soul core?!

"You shouldn't blame the people who did this to you," Cedric added with a grunt. "They effectively saved your life. That spell wouldn't have broken were it not for—" he faltered and grimaced awkwardly, hand rising to rub the back of his neck, "—well, me."

Eden blinked. Her gaze dropped to the wooden bracelet on his wrist. It was the first time she was seeing it properly. It was sturdy and plain, yet beautiful and filled with quiet grace. She stared.

There was something else there. Something that she could just about make out if she squinted hard enough. A shape that shimmered in and out of sight.

Eden reached over impulsively and touched the object. "What is that?"

They both gasped as a pendant materialized in a flash of crimson. It rose above Cedric's flesh, quivering and straining as if it wanted to escape the bracelet's hold and leap into her hand. She took a shaky breath.

It was shaped like a tree, the red light pulsing from it echoing her own heartbeat.

"Shit," Cedric mumbled. "I was right." He stared at Eden, his expression grim. "It really *is* resonating with you."

CHAPTER EIGHTEEN

Surprise widened Strickland's eyes. "What did you just say?"

Brianna gripped the glass of water on her lap.

She was in Strickland's office, at the Argonaut bureau. Malik stood by her chair, his presence comforting despite the tension she could feel emanating from him.

The Hexa sorcerer was bound to be restless. Though technically on the same side, Hexa and Argonaut were often at odds with one another, what with Argonaut having the right to investigate Hexa if they felt a crime had been committed by one of their agents. The same strained relationship existed between Argonaut and the other two agencies that governed the otherwordly, Rosen and Cabalista.

Brianna knew her being there put her at the mercy of the Argonaut director. Still, she trusted Strickland and the two angels framing him where he sat behind his desk. The rest of Morgan and Cassius's crew had spread out around the room, their enchanter Charlie finally turning up.

"My daughter Eden ran away from home last night," she repeated.

"Have you reported this to the police?" Strickland asked, concern clouding his face.

"No." Brianna met the director's stare squarely. "I can't. The incident Hexa reported to Argonaut this morning concerned Eden's best friend, Lois Serrano. Lois and her family were attacked by ghouls last night. The same ghouls that I believe killed the priest in Mission Dolores tonight. Those creatures were after my daughter."

Julia exchanged a startled glance with the rest of Morgan's team. "Ghouls?"

Morgan narrowed his eyes. "Why would ghouls be after your daughter?"

"I'm not sure," Brianna replied truthfully.

"I just remembered something," Malik confessed in the tense silence that followed. "Eden thought she was being followed by something a couple of days ago. I didn't think anything of it at the time, but I wonder if it might have been those ghouls." He faltered. "She said it was some kind of shadow."

Cassius stirred. "Ghouls share some of the same shadow manipulation abilities the Lucifugous have, although the demons' are a lot more powerful. It's how they hunt."

Brianna's knuckles whitened on the glass. The very thought of those monsters after her daughter made her feel ill.

"I'm sorry, Brianna," Malik murmured.

"Stop apologizing, Malik. None of this is your fault."

"Why did Eden run away from home?" Adrianne asked.

"We had an argument. A bad one." Brianna paused, remorse storming through her once more. "I grounded her."

Bailey made a face. "You grounded a sixteen-year-old? No wonder she scrammed."

Malik frowned at the wizard. "It wasn't as if Brianna had a choice."

"It's okay, Malik." Brianna sighed and put the untouched glass of water on Strickland's desk. "I should have talked things through with her."

"You and I both know Eden wasn't in the mood to talk that day," Malik protested. "She wouldn't be reasoned with!"

Brianna winced. "Well, I did tell her I had decided her future without her consent."

Julia arched an eyebrow. "Why is it the more I hear about this, the more I feel sorry for this kid?"

"What aren't you telling us, Brianna?" Strickland said, his tone hardening.

A bitter smile tilted Brianna's lips for a moment. *Trust Francis to get straight to the point.* She fisted her hands. *Here goes nothing.*

"Eden's soul core is bloodcursed."

Her words echoed around the office. The Argonaut director and his agents stared, shocked.

"What?!" Adrianne spluttered.

"So, I was right," Cassius said with a frown.

"That's what we sensed, back at the church?" Morgan asked the angel. "That eerie feeling was bloodcursed magic?"

Cassius nodded. "Like I said, I've only experienced it once before."

Strickland glared at Brianna. "How come you didn't inform the other agencies about this? You know the rules. All bloodcursed magic users are meant to be restrained in a secure facility for their own protection!"

"I can guess why she didn't, Francis." Cassius ran a hand through his hair, his expression troubled. "The last time the agencies did that to a bloodcursed magic user, the facility exploded after his soul core went berserk."

Surprise widened Brianna's eyes. "You were there?"

Cassius dipped his chin, a muscle twitching in his cheek. "I was the one who found that kid and brought him in. And I still regret it to this day." He sighed when he clocked Morgan and the others' uneasy looks. "The last known bloodcursed magic user was a boy called Samuel Brown. He was born in 1910, in Philadelphia. He was sequestered in an Argonaut facility when he was four years old, after Hexa charged me to locate him. Though the mages in the city had picked up on a new source of bloodcursed magic, they couldn't pinpoint its source. I was brought in to assist them. It took me a week to find him. His mother was keeping him behind several concealment spells, in the basement of their home."

Brianna's heart raced as she gazed at the angel,

stunned by this revelation. "I didn't know you were the one who found him. I read the case file from cover to cover and your name wasn't mentioned anywhere."

"That's the agencies for you," Morgan muttered darkly. "They like to pretend they hate Cassius, yet they never hesitate to use him to do their dirty work."

Malik studied Cassius warily. Strickland glanced at Morgan, his expression a mix of irritation and resignation.

"What happened to Samuel?" Zach asked.

Brianna replied in Cassius's stead. She knew this story like the back of her hand, as well as the stories of every other bloodcursed magic user who had been born in the last five hundred years.

"Despite Hexa and Argonaut's best efforts, Samuel's soul core became more unstable as he grew older. He simply…lost control one day."

"It happened at night, so there weren't as many people around as there would have been during the day," Cassius continued stiffly. "Still, ten agents died, along with Samuel."

A somber hush ensued. Brianna could tell Cassius still carried a lot of guilt about the dead child he had helped the agencies imprison. She was more convinced than ever now that coming here had been the right thing to do. Cassius and Morgan would help her find Eden and keep her safe. She was sure of it.

Charlie spoke, his tone hesitant. "I read a bit about bloodcursed magic when I was at school. It was never made clear what exactly made it so powerful."

"It's a type of magic that's different from all others,

yet somehow combines their abilities," Cassius said. "And, for some reason no one knows, the only magic users who seem able to detect it accurately are mages." His expression grew awkward. "And, well, me."

"Imagine someone who can wield sorcery, witchcraft, mage magic, enchantment magic, warlock magic, and more," Brianna explained. "That's how devastatingly strong bloodcursed magic is. No one has ever been able to fully assess what a bloodcursed magic user can do. But one thing is certain. The pressure of hosting that amount of magic is too much for a human soul core to bear."

"It has long been hypothesized that the Fall triggered some kind of mutation in the inherent magic that lives inside humans," Strickland said stiffly. "We believe that mutation can be passed down the bloodlines but doesn't manifest in every person who inherits it. It came to be called bloodcursed for that very reason. Like a scourge, it can skip several generations before coming to light in an unsuspecting soul." He frowned at Brianna. "No bloodcursed magic user has ever survived past their tenth birthday. Eden is sixteen. How is that possible?"

Brianna hesitated.

"She bound her daughter's magic," Cassius said quietly.

Brianna met the angel's steady gaze, not surprised that he'd figured it out.

The air became fraught with tension as Adrianne, Bailey, and Charlie exchanged dismayed looks. A muscle jumped in Strickland's jawline.

"Binding a human's soul core is illegal, Brianna!" the director snapped. "It's a crime that carries a heavy punishment. Hexa and the other agencies will have to be made aware of—"

"Hexa knows," Brianna said tiredly.

"What?" Adrianne said dully in the stunned silence.

"My uncle was the head of Hexa at the time I was pregnant with Eden. He was like a father to me and considered Eden his granddaughter." An uncommon surge of bravado rose inside Brianna then. She tilted her chin defiantly at Strickland. "Hexa had long speculated that the way to save a bloodcursed magic user from their fated death was for a powerful mage to bind their soul core from birth. It would mean the bloodcursed magic user would never be able to access their magic, but at least they would be saved from premature death. The Hexa mages who were around at the time of Samuel Brown's confinement wrote of their attempts to do just that. They failed. But we—me and the Hexa mages who were willing to help my uncle when Eden was born—succeeded. Eden's bloodcursed soul core was spellbound a few hours after her birth with my witch magic and that of the most powerful Hexa mages of the time."

Strickland's expression grew thunderous. "Are you telling me that Hexa committed this crime fully knowing the consequences of their actions? And that they deliberately hid it from the other agencies?!"

"All agencies have skeletons in their closets they'd rather not reveal to outsiders, Francis," Brianna said grimly. "We don't talk about them, but everyone knows they're there."

"That we do," Zach muttered darkly.

Brianna glanced at the demon. He evidently still held some lingering bitterness from his past dealings with Hexa, Rosen, and Cabalista.

"So, you mean to tell me everything's been fine since then?" Strickland asked Brianna in disbelief. "That there were no repercussions?!"

Brianna's heart grew leaden at his questions, her defiance fading as quickly as it had appeared. It was a moment before she could speak.

"I won't lie to you, Francis. Putting a spell on Eden's soul had consequences none of us saw coming." She met his gaze steadily. "I've not been able to touch my own daughter since her birth. I should have told her about her spellbound magic when she was old enough to understand what I had done. Maybe our relationship would have been the better for it. But now she's gone. And I may never get to explain my actions to her."

CHAPTER NINETEEN

MORGAN PRESSED THE BUTTON FOR THE ELEVATOR. Cassius followed him inside when the doors slid open, his face drawn. The cabin rose swiftly, taking them from the underground garage to the upper floors of the high-rise. Morgan glanced at Cassius, troubled.

The Empyreal had been quiet since they left Argonaut.

Morgan knew Brianna's confession weighed heavily on Cassius's mind. He hadn't known about Cassius's past involvement with a bloodcursed magic user until tonight.

Then again, there are still many things I don't know about Cassius.

That it had been a child he had tracked down and who had eventually died was something Morgan suspected Cassius had never forgiven himself for. And now, the fate of another lay in his hands. Though he would have preferred Argonaut not accept Brianna's request to find her daughter, Morgan knew Strickland had no choice in the matter. They had to stop the ghouls hunting the girl. And he was certain Cassius would forge ahead to find and save Eden Monroe even if Argonaut had refused to assist Brianna, regardless of Morgan's own wishes that he not get involved in a case that was bound to hurt him all over again.

Strickland hadn't arrested Brianna and had let her go on the condition that she cooperate with the investigation Argonaut would have to initiate with regards to Hexa spellbinding Eden Monroe's soul sixteen years ago.

"Just help me find my daughter, Francis," Brianna had said, desperation adding an edge to her words. "I'll do anything you want." She'd turned to Cassius and Morgan. "Something happened tonight. Something that broke the spell trapping Eden's magic. We need to get to her before someone else does, and before her soul core becomes unstable again." She'd gazed beseechingly at Cassius. "The only people in the city right now who can detect her magic are you, me, and, for some reason I still don't understand, those ghouls. Please, help me save my daughter, Cassius!"

Morgan understood the urgency behind Brianna's request. A bloodcursed magic user could be a deadly weapon in the wrong hands. The ghouls had to be acting under someone else's direction; the creatures weren't intelligent enough to know what to do with a bloodcursed magic user. Whoever sent them after Eden must know about the young girl's hidden magic. Which meant Hexa probably had a mole.

"There's a chance the agencies will decide to keep

her captive if we find her," Cassius had told Brianna somberly. "Will you be able to live with that if they do?"

Brianna had swallowed at his words, her face gaunt and her eyes dark with regret. "I just want her back alive."

They exited the elevator on the penthouse floor, Cassius's steps heavy as they approached his apartment. He unlocked his front door. A surprised look danced across his face when Morgan dropped a kiss on his temple and started walking away.

"Aren't you coming in?"

"I'll grab a shower and a change of clothes at my place first. Why don't you go ahead and get ready for bed?"

Cassius hesitated. "Okay."

Morgan kicked off his boots in the hallway of his apartment and stripped out of his clothes on the way to his bedroom, his mind full of the man he had just parted company with. Though he'd wanted nothing more than to take Cassius in his arms and tell him everything was going to be okay, he didn't have the right to make promises he couldn't keep. Besides, Cassius needed some space right now.

He'd just turned the shower on and stepped under the hot spray when light footsteps sounded behind him. Strong arms wrapped around his waist. A warm, naked body pressed against his back.

Morgan twisted around. "Cassius?"

Cassius rose and pressed his mouth to his, his cheeks flushed and his eyes molten gray with need. Morgan's pulse quickened, lust instantly flooding his veins. He cradled Cassius's face in his hands and deepened the kiss, the angel welcoming his tongue with a soft moan and a breathy sound.

There were times when Cassius got like this. When he got needy and initiated their lovemaking. More often than not, it was when the darkness inside him got to be too much. When five hundred years of unhappy memories and loneliness came crashing down upon him.

In those moments, Morgan became the anchor he sought. The person who could ground him and carry him through the darkness and into the light. The one being who could make him lose himself in pleasure so fierce it purged him of all his bad thoughts and his insecurities and regrets.

It was a role Morgan gladly accepted. One he embraced with open arms and cherished above all else. That this man, this angel who was the most powerful among the otherworldly, would come to him in his moments of weakness and seek his heat to make him forget this cruel world was Cassius's unspoken confession of love to him. And so Morgan gave it his all. He took Cassius to bed and surrendered his body, his heart, and his soul to the angel in his arms, his every touch and kiss an admission of his own feelings for the beguiling Empyreal.

Cassius's pants and moans echoed sweetly in Morgan's ears as Morgan worshipped him with his hands, lips, and tongue, Cassius's own fingers urgent on Morgan's flesh and in his hair. His breath hitched when Morgan finally went down on him, his cock trembling and weeping on Morgan's tongue, his heels digging into Morgan's back.

Morgan's dick throbbed painfully where it pressed into the mattress. He focused on Cassius and bobbed his head up and down his hot shaft from the root to the tip, his hands fixing the angel's dancing hips as he writhed and arched on the bed, taking his time to blow him slow and deep. The powerful sucking motions of his mouth and jaw soon brought Cassius to an explosive climax, the angel's harsh cries loud in the dark bedroom, his orgasm making the connection between their soul cores spark with fire. Savage satisfaction coursed through Morgan as he swallowed the hot cum flooding his throat, his gaze locked on Cassius's pleasure-glazed eyes as the angel looked down his shuddering body at him, fingers clenched tightly in Morgan's hair.

"Show me." Morgan dropped a kiss on the tip of Cassius's half-hard cock as he let him go, his voice a low growl. "Show me what you want me to do to you, Cassius."

Cassius shivered, his expression feverish. He bit his lip and rolled onto his front, body trembling and sweat-slicked skin flushed. A feral smile twisted Morgan's mouth as Cassius spread his legs for him. He loved this side of Cassius. When he stopped being coy and demanded pleasure.

Cassius's hands twisted in the sheets as Morgan parted his butt cheeks, exposing his most sinful part. He sucked in air and arched his head off the mattress at the first flick of Morgan's tongue against his opening.

"Ah!"

Cassius's guttural cry made Morgan want to plunge his dick inside him there and then. He clamped down on the animal urge to take the man lying pliantly beneath him and rimmed him instead, prepping him for his penetration.

Cassius's breathing grew ragged and the sounds he made more broken as Morgan stretched him deliciously open with his tongue. Morgan waited until Cassius's entrance had softened before drawing him onto his hands and knees. He poured lube onto Cassius's quivering hole, coated his own cock liberally, and dropped the bottle on the bed. Cassius shuddered as Morgan took hold of his hips and pressed the broad head of his dick to his entrance.

They both groaned as Morgan sank into Cassius's heat inch by slow inch. Morgan gnashed his teeth and pushed in all the way to the hilt, perilously close to coming as Cassius gripped him tightly, his insides fitting snuggly around Morgan. He pulled back and punched forward, his shaft sliding over the swollen bump of Cassius's prostate.

"Yesss!" Cassius moaned. His fingers found the headboard and his hips rocked against Morgan's cock as Morgan set the pace of their lovemaking. "More! Harder!"

Morgan curled one hand in Cassius's hair and yanked his head back until his spine bowed beautifully, his grunts matching his powerful thrusts. Cassius submitted to his rough hold, the way his body tightened around Morgan telling him he loved the savage play.

Morgan squeezed his eyes shut and bit his lip, pleasure storming him as he plunged in and out of Cassius, giving him what they both so desperately wanted, the tightness in his balls and the tension in his spine heralding his own orgasm.

Cassius stiffened and cried out a moment later, his back passage grasping Morgan's cock hard. Morgan cursed as Cassius convulsed around him, his insides throbbing and spasming fiercely on Morgan's shaft, his own cock painting the sheet with his cum.

Morgan finally lost control, fingers biting into Cassius's flesh and body surrendering to its base instinct as he rutted wildly against the angel. He came on a loud shout, his climax so fierce he felt dizzy, his cock pulsing deep inside Cassius's welcoming heat.

They collapsed on the bed a moment later, Morgan still buried inside Cassius.

"More," Cassius mumbled, squeezing Morgan's half-hard cock with his hole. He grasped Morgan's hand and turned his head to meet his gaze as he kissed his knuckles. "I want more!"

This time, Morgan read pure desire in Cassius's stormy eyes and color-stained cheekbones. Gone was the darkness and sorrow he had felt in Cassius's first kiss. Cassius wanted him and him only.

Morgan shuddered, pulled his swelling arousal out of Cassius, and flipped him on his back. Cassius's thighs found his hips as he thrust back inside the angel's eager body. He clutched desperately at

Morgan's back with his hands and sank his heels into Morgan's ass, anchoring them together as he rolled his hips and met Morgan's thrusts, his expression wanton.

Morgan took Cassius's mouth and swallowed his gasps and cries, his chest tight with emotion and his body drowning in pleasure, Cassius's scent filling his head while fire resonated between their soul cores.

CHAPTER TWENTY

THE SCREECH OF SEAGULLS WOKE EDEN FROM A RESTLESS sleep. She stirred and winced before raising a hand to shield her eyes from the bright sunlight. She sat up slowly, her mouth dry and her mind dulled by tiredness.

Her dreams had been plagued by shadowy monsters intent on killing her.

Eden ran a hand through her hair and looked around. She froze, stomach lurching. Cedric was gone, the dirty mattress he'd laid on empty.

Panic flooded Eden and sent her heart hammering against her ribs. Something rustled under her fingers as she scrambled onto her hands and knees. She sagged when she saw the note Cedric had left her, relief making her weak. She picked it up.

Cedric's handwriting was as rigid as he was, his script flawless and his language formal. His message was brief; he'd gone out to get them breakfast. A reluctant smile tugged at her lips as she studied the perfectly formed letters inked across the paper.

He really is an old soul.

Eden got up and went to the washroom Cedric had shown her the night before. They hadn't spoken much after he'd told her the pendant attached to his bracelet was somehow resonating with her magic. He'd ordered her to get some sleep and had kept watch for most of the night, his brooding gaze sweeping over Eden when he thought she wasn't looking.

She pressed a hand to her stomach as she observed her reflection in the cracked mirror above the dirty sink.

I can't believe I have magic.

She'd thought she would feel different. Better, somehow. But she didn't. Bar the vague sensation of something warm deep inside her, nothing had changed.

Rainwater had collected in a butt next to a broken window. Eden splashed some on her face and ran her fingers through her disheveled hair before tying it in a knot at the base of her neck. She grimaced, recalling the backpack full of supplies she'd left back at the hostel.

I wonder if he'll let me retrieve it.

Eden gave herself a final glance in the mirror before exiting the washroom, hoping she looked more mature than her sixteen years. Her ears grew warm as she headed back to where they'd sought refuge for the night.

Not that I care what he thinks of me.

Her best friend's face rose before her eyes. She wondered what Lois would make of Cedric.

I should call her when I get a chance.

She sobered immediately. She couldn't tell Lois what had happened last night. She probably wouldn't believe her anyway.

Eden grew steadily despondent as she waited for Cedric to return. All her carefully made plans had gone out of the window. Months of arduous work and prudent scheming had vanished down the drain in an instant, leaving her adrift and without purpose. She'd thought, if it was going to come to that, that running away from home would be the hardest thing she would ever have to do in her life. Yet, here she was, on the run from monsters and with newly awakened magic, in the company of a stranger she still didn't trust.

Heat flared inside her, a hot spot in her belly. Eden blinked, startled.

"I wasn't sure what you liked, so I got you a bacon muffin and an egg one."

She twisted around. Cedric was walking up to her, a large paper bag and a two-cup drinks holder in hand.

Eden hadn't heard him come in. Her gaze dropped to his bracelet, realization dawning. But she had *felt* him, in another way, her magic reacting to the invisible pendant.

Though the eerie phenomenon should have scared her, Eden didn't feel any fear. Instead, she found herself experiencing a strange sense of companionship, as if she and the pendant belonged together, somehow.

Surprise shot through her when she saw what Cedric was carrying on his shoulder.

"My backpack!" Eden climbed to her feet and rushed over to him. "How did you get it out of the hostel?!"

He handed her the bag and watched as she opened it and looked inside. "I used an illusion spell to take on your appearance. And breaking into that locker was child's play."

Eden's hands stilled on the backpack. Her eyed rounded. "You what?!"

Cedric sighed. He murmured an incantation under his breath, his pupils flaring jade green for a moment. Eden stumbled back a step as he transformed into an exact replica of her, his frame shrinking.

No, not exact.

Her heart thumped in her chest.

Cedric's version of her looked ten times more refined and poised than she could ever be, blue eyes calm and not a strand of hair out of place.

Eden stared. *Is this how he sees me?*

Cedric released the spell and sat cross-legged on the floor. "Come, let's eat."

Eden's stomach grumbled loudly as he emptied out the contents of the paper bag. She flushed and lowered herself opposite him. Though she had energy bars in her bag, the breakfast muffins looked and smelled delicious. They ate in silence, Cedric wolfing down three sandwiches all by himself. He grimaced when he took a sip of his coffee.

"I still can't get used to this drink of yours," he muttered.

Eden paused, her hot chocolate halfway to her mouth. "What do you normally drink?"

"Honeysuckle and Angel Ivy tea."

Eden stared, her pulse now racing for a whole other reason. "I've been meaning to ask you this. You're not… from around here, are you?"

She waved a vague hand at their surroundings.

Cedric smirked, his cheeks dimpling. "Are you asking me if I'm an alien?"

Eden's pulse stuttered. Serious Cedric was handsome as sin. Smiling Cedric was on a whole other level.

She told her fluttering heart to calm the heck down and narrowed her eyes at him. "You know full well what I'm asking."

Cedric downed his coffee, made a face, and crumpled the paper cup. "No, I am not from this realm."

Eden held her breath and waited for him to continue. She frowned when he didn't. "That's it? You're not going to tell me anything else?" Her voice grew shrill despite her best efforts to stay calm. "Like what that pendant is and why you were there last night, in that cemetery? Or how you know I have bloodcursed magic in me?!"

Her words echoed around the room, loud and full of frustration. Eden bit her lip, surprised at her own outburst. She fisted her hands.

No, I have every right to ask him these questions. I've

been kept in the dark too long. First by my mother and Hexa, and now by him. I'm not taking any more of their bullshit!

Cedric studied her moodily. Eden had a feeling he wasn't that bothered by her angry accusations. Instead, he seemed to be mulling over something, just like he'd done all night.

"I will tell you more," he said reluctantly. "But first, I have to check something out."

Eden stared as he climbed to his feet.

He offered her his hand, his expression almost friendly. "Come on, let's get out of here."

Eden hesitated before taking it. Heat danced across her fingertips and up her arm when they touched. Her ears grew hot as he pulled her up, awareness rippling through her. Cedric grabbed his weathered leather bag and headed for the exit, a frown marring his brow for a moment, as if he'd sensed the electricity between them and didn't like it one bit.

Eden shouldered her backpack and headed after him, now more than a little confused. "Where are we going?"

"To see someone in Chinatown."

CHAPTER TWENTY-ONE

Lois Serrano's lower lip trembled as she stared at Cassius and Morgan, apprehension darkening her eyes.

"It's okay, Lois," Malik said gently. "These men won't hurt you."

He glanced at them, a warning look flashing on his face.

Cassius bit back a sigh. The way the sorcerer was frowning at them, they might as well be child killers. Gary Serrano, Lois's father, hovered anxiously next to his daughter's bed, his hand clenched atop his walking stick and his expression equally wary.

Brianna had opted not to accompany Cassius and Morgan to the hospital, worried her presence would stop Eden's best friend from talking. Cassius had to agree with her reasoning. The kid was jumpy as heck and definitely hiding something.

The mages stationed on the magic ward at San Francisco Memorial had done a great job patching up the Serranos. Considering how badly they'd been mauled by the ghouls, it was a miracle they were even alive. Had Brianna not brought a medical mage with her the morning she went to the Serranos' house, they would likely not have survived their trip to the hospital.

Cassius caught a glimpse of a small, dark-haired boy sitting in bed with Helen Serrano in the private room across the corridor. Though awake, Lois's mother still looked pale as she held her son. Brianna had been told the Serranos' injuries wouldn't leave them with permanent physical scars. As for the psychological ones, they would likely carry those dark memories to their graves.

Cassius and Morgan had decided to split their team up that morning. Julia and Zach were assisting Lambert and Willis on the bank robberies case, while Adrianne and Bailey had taken over Zakir Singh's investigation of the ghoul attack at Presidio Heights and the cemetery in Mission Dolores. Charlie was back in the tech lab with the Altered Mind box. The enchanter had told Cassius and Morgan he was close to a breakthrough when they'd parted ways last night.

As for the elusive Usman Abbas, he was still nowhere to be found.

Cassius pulled a chair over to the bed and sat down. "Hi, Lois. My name is Cassius. This is Morgan."

He indicated the Aerial. Morgan dipped his head at Lois and her father. The way Lois flushed slightly as she looked at Morgan told Cassius his lover had just unwittingly broken another heart. He suppressed the torrid images of their lovemaking from that morning and concentrated on the young girl in front of him.

"Do you remember what happened the night of the attack?"

Lois hesitated before nodding. "Some of it. I was about to go to bed when I heard a noise on the roof. I opened my window and took a look outside but couldn't see anything. That's when I heard glass shatter somewhere in the house."

Her hands fisted in the covers.

Gary Serrano placed a reassuring hand on his daughter's shoulder. "It's okay, sweetheart."

Lois nodded tremulously at her father before taking a shaky breath. "I ran to my brother's room. Something was there. It was dark and I—I couldn't see clearly." She stopped and swallowed. "I just knew that, whatever it was, it was going to kill him."

Cassius had read the reports from Hexa and Singh. Lois Serrano had singlehandedly saved her brother's life.

Eden has a great friend.

It made him more curious to meet Brianna's daughter. He could tell she was someone special, just from the way Brianna and Malik spoke about her. Though the relationship between Brianna and Eden was fraught, there was no denying the witch loved her daughter and would do anything in her power to protect her.

"The creatures that attacked you were ghouls,"

Morgan told Lois and her father. "They are evil, flesh-eating spirits from the Nine Hells. They rarely wander into this realm but, for some reason we still haven't figured out, there appears to be a pack of them in San Francisco right now."

Lois paled. Gary Serrano stiffened.

"They are after Eden," Cassius explained. "There was another attack last night, in Mission Dolores. A priest was killed and there's evidence of a fight involving magic. We believe Eden was there."

"What?!" Lois mumbled, stunned. "But—but why would those…those things be after Eden?!"

"Because she has powerful magic."

Malik straightened, lines marring his brow. "We shouldn't be telling them this."

"On the contrary," Cassius retorted. "The more Lois is aware of what's going on, the more likely she is to tell us what she knows about Eden's plans."

"Still, we need to run this by Brianna and Hexa," the sorcerer argued.

"Keeping secrets from Eden is what landed Brianna in this mess in the first place." Morgan grunted. "You guys need to learn to be a bit more honest with the people you're trying to protect."

Cassius met Lois's shocked gaze. "We suspect those ghouls followed Eden to your place that night. And now they're after her again and will continue chasing her until they find her. We need to get to her first."

"But Edie doesn't have magic!" Lois said. "She said so herself. That's why her mother hates her and Hexa treats her so badly."

Malik's expression grew pained. "Is that what Eden told you?"

Lois hesitated before nodding. "She knows you and your people look down on her because she lacks magic. That's why she couldn't understand why her mom insisted on her attending Saint Helena. It seemed utterly pointless to her. She thought it was just another way for Brianna and Hexa to torture her."

"Lois," Gary Serrano murmured, upset.

Cassius could see Lois's father shared his daughter's sentiments to an extent. He swallowed a sigh. Things were even worse than he'd anticipated. From everything he'd heard so far, Eden Monroe had had every reason to run away from home if she'd felt that way all her life.

"I don't dislike Eden's mom," Lois murmured, staring at her hands. "She's always been kind to me." She looked up at Malik. "And so have you and the other Hexa agents I've met at Eden's house. It always puzzled me how you could be so nice to me but go out of your way to avoid Eden. None of it made sense. But Edie… she couldn't see that. Once she was old enough to realize why she was being shunned, she shut herself off from all of you." Her tone turned accusing. "It was awful to see Edie like that. I was worried she would do something silly one day. That's why I decided to help her. I wanted to make sure she'd be safe after she got away from you."

A muscle jumped in Malik's jawline. Cassius could tell the sorcerer was devastated by Lois's words.

"Will you tell us what you know about Eden's plans?"

Lois's knuckles whitened on her lap. She lifted her chin, her expression growing heated as she met Cassius's gaze squarely. "What will you do if you find Eden? Will you take her back to Brianna and Hexa?"

"I'm not going to lie to you," Cassius said quietly in the stilted silence. "There's a good chance the agencies that govern the otherworldly and magic users will decide Eden needs to be kept in a secure facility for the rest of her life, as much to save her as to protect the rest of us. That's what Brianna has been trying to avoid for the past sixteen years."

Lois's eyes widened. "What? But why?!"

"Because Eden's magic is not only incredibly powerful, it is also unstable," Morgan said. "Truth be told, Eden should technically have died years ago. The only thing that's kept her alive is the spell Brianna and a group of Hexa mages cast on her when she was born, to bind the magic inside her body. If we don't find her soon, there's a chance her soul core will explode and kill her and those around her."

Tears swam in Lois's eyes as she stared at them, her expression bereft. She sagged, her body shrinking on the bed.

Her father hugged her and stroked her hair. "It's okay, sweetie. I'm here."

Lois clutched at his shirt, her breath hitching as she swallowed a sob.

"Will you help us find Eden and keep her safe, Lois?" Cassius said.

It was a moment before Lois spoke. She clenched her jaw and lifted her head from her father's chest, determination filling her face. "Promise me that you'll let me see her when you find her. And that you'll listen to her wishes."

Cassius nodded. "I promise."

They left the private ward moments later, their pace brisk.

"I can't believe Eden bought fake ID on the dark web and opened another bank account," Malik muttered, aghast.

"You guys didn't give her much of a choice," Morgan said with a grunt. "The fact that she'd been planning this for so long makes it clear she thought she would need an escape route one day. I would have scrammed years ago."

Cassius glanced at Morgan, a smile tugging at his lips.

"What?" Morgan said.

"Nothing. I was just trying to imagine you as a hotheaded human teenager. I bet you would have raised hell and broken hearts everywhere you went."

Morgan arched an eyebrow, a devilish smile stretching his mouth. "Would I have broken yours?"

Cassius's breath caught in his throat.

"Maybe," he mumbled.

Morgan's grin widened. "I'm pretty sure you would have broken mine."

Malik glanced between them, his expression stern. "Are you two flirting right now?"

"No, we're not," Cassius said firmly. "There's a

youth hostel in Mission Dolores, close to that church. We drove past it last night, when we left the cemetery. We should check it out."

They bumped into Charlie when they exited the elevator in the underground garage under the hospital.

Excitement gleamed in the enchanter's eyes as he crossed the floor toward them. "I have news."

CHAPTER TWENTY-TWO

Eden observed the murky alley Cedric had just turned into, her heart full of misgivings. The hustle and bustle of Grant Avenue faded behind her as she headed after him.

They'd spent most of the morning moving furtively across town, Cedric taking a convoluted route to their destination while sticking to crowded places they could easily lose themselves in. He'd refused to tell her exactly where they were going or whom they were going to see. If it weren't for the fact that he'd saved her life and knew something about her bloodcursed magic, Eden would have dumped his stubborn ass.

Graffiti-covered doors and dumpsters lined the passageway they'd entered. Steam from vents and air conditioning units swirled around the fire escapes rising up the back walls of the buildings crowding a narrow strip of sky. Eden tensed slightly as they passed several people sleeping on the ground and a makeshift cardboard tent where a homeless man sat reading a paper, his dog on his lap. The animal growled when it saw them. Cedric glanced at it, eyes narrowing for a moment.

The dog whimpered and burrowed its head in its master's chest.

Eden swallowed a sigh. *Great. Now he's scaring small animals.*

The more time she spent with Cedric, the more of a mystery he became. She couldn't deny that she found him attractive. She would have to be dead not to. And she knew he cared for her, in his own awkward way. He wouldn't have saved her life if he didn't. Still, she wished he would just tell her what the heck was going on.

She'd gone a couple of steps before she realized he wasn't with her. Eden stopped and turned.

Cedric was standing under a narrow porch, in front of a door with flaking, dark blue paint and a cracked glass panel. *"Mr. Lee's Gift Emporium and Rare Antiquities - Best in Chinatown!"* was written on the red sign above it in garish, dirty white letters. Cedric muttered something under his breath, twisted the handle, and headed inside. Eden hesitated before following him.

The door closed behind them with a clack, the chimes hanging off the top of the frame ringing with a joviality that didn't match the murky interior. It took a few seconds for her eyes to adjust to the gloom. Cedric was already forging ahead, his steps sure as he navigated a cramped corridor between the tightly packed display cabinets that lined the wooden floor, their shelves crowded with merchandise.

Eden stared distractedly at the strange objects mounted on the walls and overspilling the racks as she hastened her pace and went after him. Low voices reached them when they neared the back of the shop. They turned a corner and slowed to a stop.

"Oh, *come on*, man! That Rolex is worth at least six grand. You gotta give me more than that!"

A skinny guy in a dark top and jogging bottoms that hung perilously low on his hips was leaning on a counter protected by glass and metal bars. He wiped the sweat pouring down his face with a dirty handkerchief, one leg bobbing jerkily, his body twitching as if in the grip of a fever.

Eden could tell he was high on something.

A black man in a wine-red kaftan stood behind the cash register. He had long white hair knotted in dreadlocks and the bluest eyes Eden had ever seen.

He glanced their way and handed the watch he'd been examining to the twitching man, his face impassive. "I'm afraid I can't, Tony. This is clearly a fake."

Skinny Guy deflated like a lead balloon. "But the dude I sto—I mean I got it from looked like the real deal," he whined. "It's gotta be worth at least two grand, even if it's a fake!"

"Five hundred bucks is all I'm willing to give you," Dreadlocks stated firmly. "Take it or leave it."

Skinny Guy cursed before shoving the watch back at Dreadlocks. "Just hand me the damn money!"

Dreadlocks took the Rolex, opened the cash register, and gave him a wad of bills. "Make sure you spend this on food and rent, Tony." He clutched the money, briefly resisting the other man's attempt to snatch it out of his hand. "You should lay off those happy pills."

"Fuck you," Skinny Guy grumbled.

He shoved the money in his pocket, bumped into Cedric, and stormed toward the exit.

Cedric gave Skinny Guy a dark look as he vanished around the corner. He dusted off his shoulder, mild revulsion reflected in his eyes.

"Really, Galliad?" he told Dreadlocks. "'Best in Chinatown?'"

Dreadlocks winced. "I would prefer it if you referred to me as Brian, Your Highness." He paused and scratched his cheek. "By the way, you realize Tony just swiped something from your pocket, right?"

Cedric froze. He patted his jeans.

Eden blinked. *Your Highness?!*

"Why, that—!" Cedric dropped his bag and took off after Skinny Guy. He returned a second later and pointed an accusing finger at Eden. "You, don't move an inch from there!" He twisted around and disappeared at a dead run.

Eden frowned. "Jeez, he really has an attitude problem."

She became conscious of an inquisitive stare.

Dreadlocks was gazing at her with open curiosity. "It's rare to see Cedric in the company of a girl. You must be pretty special to have caught his eye."

Eden flushed. "We're not together. I mean, we're together, but not in *that* way."

Dreadlocks grinned. "Something tells me you wish it were that way."

"Heck no!" Eden scoffed. "That guy is prickly as hell and a stubborn ass to boot!"

Dreadlocks laughed. "You're right about that." He unlocked the opening on the counter and came out, his kaftan swishing around his legs. "My name is Galliad Fenhorn, although I prefer to go by Brian in this realm."

Eden hesitated. *He must be from the same place as Cedric.*

"I'm…Eden."

Galliad raised an eyebrow. "Just Eden?"

She nodded awkwardly.

Galliad's expression grew less teasing. "It's nice to meet you, mysterious Eden."

He offered her his hand. Eden shook it, her fingers easily swallowed by his large grasp. Heat shot up her arm, startling her.

Galliad stiffened and sucked in air, his eyes brightening to a dazzling sapphire. "Bloody hellfire!"

CHAPTER TWENTY-THREE

CEDRIC ENTERED THE SHOP, LOCKED THE FRONT DOOR, and twisted the *Open* sign hanging off the frame to *Closed*. He cast a careful look at the alleyway outside before heading for the back of the shop.

He'd caught up with Tony one alley over and recovered his wallet intact. The guy had pulled a knife on him but had dropped it and disappeared with a horrified scream when Cedric had cast a weak spell bomb at his feet.

Lines wrinkled Cedric's brow. *I hope the ghouls don't pick up a trace of my magic.*

He'd done his best to try and mix his and Eden's scents with the crowds milling around the city while they were making their way over to Galliad's shop. It would only buy them so much time, but time was very much of the essence right now. He had questions and Galliad was the only one he trusted would have the answers.

He stopped when he came in sight of the counter and cash register. Eden was gone, as was his bag.

"We're in here, Your Highness," a voice called out faintly from his left.

Cedric leveled a frown at the camera in the corner of the ceiling and made for a shabby curtain masking a metal door. It was unlocked.

He found Galliad and a pale-faced Eden seated in a small kitchen beyond. A fawn-colored pug was perched on her lap. The dog eyed Cedric beadily as he closed the door.

"You're the second prince of the Dryad kingdom?!" Eden said hoarsely, her eyes round with shock and her tone faintly accusing.

Cedric grimaced at Galliad. "What else have you told her in the five minutes I've been gone?"

Galliad poured a third cup of tea from a pretty porcelain pot, his expression unrepentant. "Oh, not much. Here, why don't you have a seat, Your Highness? I brewed your favorite."

Longing danced through Cedric, the familiar scent of honeysuckle and Angel Ivy teasing his nostrils. It reminded him of home and long afternoons spent with his mother and brothers in the palace garden. He reluctantly took the chair Galliad indicated and lifted the dainty cup to his lips.

"I would prefer it if you didn't address me by that title."

The first sip of the sweet tea almost made him groan. It had been forever since he'd tasted it. It made him willing to forgive Galliad anything in that moment.

"The habit of a few hundred years is hard to relinquish, my Prince," Galliad said gallantly.

Cedric rolled his eyes. "You've been on Earth almost as long as I was slumbering, Galliad."

"Wait." Eden's gaze shifted from Galliad to Cedric, her expression suspicious. "Just how old are you guys?!"

"I'm three hundred years old." Cedric pointed at Galliad. "He's over fifteen hundred years old."

Eden gaped. The pug pressed its forelegs against her chest and licked her chin. She stroked it distractedly.

"I am but a sapling," Galliad murmured. "Dryads are long-lived," he explained at her stunned expression. "Our lifespan extends to thousands of human years. We spend the first three hundred years or so of it in the ground, maturing until we can assume our adult humanoid form. Like all royalty, His Highness here came of age faster." He indicated Cedric. "But he only awoke from his dormant phase a relatively short while ago."

Eden stared at them blindly before looking into her drink.

"I've read a little about Dryads," she mumbled. "Nowhere did it say that your life span stretches to thousands of years or that you actually grow like—well, trees in the ground."

Galliad shrugged. "A lot of what is written in the human history books about Dryads is fake."

"And whose fault is that?" Cedric muttered.

Galliad smiled. Eden chewed her lip.

"Whatever burning question is struggling to escape you, you should get it off your chest," Galliad drawled.

Eden's ears grew red. Cedric stared at her, puzzled.

"Hmm, well, I was kind of wondering how you," she shrugged awkwardly, "you know—"

Galliad's smile widened, blue eyes sparkling with delight. "If you mean how do we reproduce, it's the same way all species do. We mate. Dryad babies look just like human ones before they grow into a tree." He chuckled. "And the cutest baby our kingdom has seen in the last few hundred years is without a doubt our young prince here."

"Oh, please," Cedric scoffed into his tea, his ears hot.

He glanced furtively at Eden. *I can't believe she actually asked him how Dryads mate!*

He told himself the flutter in his stomach had nothing to do with the human girl sitting across the way from him. A frown marred his brow as he recalled the spark he'd felt back at the warehouse and the heat between them the night before, when they'd touched.

That was just static electricity, nothing more.

The voice inside him, the one that sounded just like his beloved older brother, laughed at that.

"So, is the reason you've come to see me because Eden here has bloodcursed magic?" Galliad said mildly.

"How the hell do you know that?" Cedric scowled at Eden. "Did you tell him?!"

"No!" she denied guiltily. "I—I think he detected it when he shook my hand."

"No need to have a go at the girl, Your Highness," Galliad murmured. "It is as young Eden said."

"Damn it." Cedric ran a hand through his hair, annoyed at himself for snapping at Eden. "Well, I guess it doesn't matter. I was intending to ask him about your magic anyway." He gave Galliad a jaundiced look. "I keep forgetting you're my father's Head Mage."

Galliad waved a vague hand. "Now, now. I passed that mantle to Elwyn ages ago."

"Elwyn is good and my father values his counsel, but we're all waiting for you to return, Galliad."

Galliad scratched his cheek. "I don't think she's forgiven me yet."

Cedric narrowed his eyes at the Dryad mage. "Are you seriously telling me you refuse to return to our kingdom still because of your marital problems?"

"Thalia has a long memory," Galliad muttered.

"You had an argument with your wife?" Eden asked hesitantly.

"She threatened me with her sword, no less."

"Thalia is one of the Dryad kingdom's generals," Cedric explained at Eden's confused look.

"Oh."

"So, why are you here, my Prince?" Galliad said, his tone growing serious. "And why have you brought me a bloodcursed magic user?"

Cedric sighed. "Because we need to inform my father of what's happening. And because of what I'm about to show you." He paused. "Can you shield this room?"

Galliad nodded, curious. He murmured a spell

under his breath, his eyes glowing briefly. Dryad magic pulsed across the kitchen, forming a bubble that would block out any other magic.

Cedric reached across the table, took a startled Eden's hand, and brought her fingers to his bracelet. Crimson light bloomed into existence, bathing the room red. The air sizzled with power. The pug whined, jumped off Eden's lap, and ran under the table.

The tree pendant materialized out of thin air, the wooden piece vibrating as if trying to leap into Eden's grasp.

Galliad cursed and jumped to his feet, the chair clattering to the floor behind him. "What the hell is that doing here?! It should be under lock and key, in our kingdom's treasury!" He glowered at Cedric. "Is this why you've come to Earth? Because you have this cursed thing with you?!"

"Cursed?" Eden repeated, wide-eyed.

"That pendant is the Bloodcursed Devilwood Summoning Staff, an artifact of great power." A muscle jumped in Galliad's jawline. "It is imperative that it doesn't fall in the wrong hands." He folded his arms across his chest and studied Cedric with a flinty look. "Well, Your Highness? Would you care to explain what *that* is doing out of our kingdom's treasury? Does His Majesty even know it's no longer in Ivory Peaks?!"

"Yes," Cedric said in a tired voice. "It was my father, the king, who sent me here. The palace was attacked by an unknown enemy a year ago. Several guards died but we managed to keep the intruders out of the treasury. My father believed their target was this staff. The court seer confirmed his suspicions. She advised him to send the weapon to Earth, along with me."

Galliad slowly pulled up the chair and sat down, a frown still darkening his brow. "Why in the name of the Nine Hells would Regina recommend such a foolish plan?"

"She told us of a vision she had following the attack. That there would be a battle in this realm, one that would affect the future of all realms. She said the staff would be needed to defeat the enemy here, on Earth. She spoke of allies we had yet to meet. And she instructed me to guard the staff until such a time came when the one who can wield it appeared before me."

They both looked at Eden.

She drew a sharp breath. "Wait. You're saying *I'm* the one who can use this thing?! No way!"

Cedric dipped his chin. "Indeed I am. I wouldn't have been drawn to follow you and battle those ghouls in the park and the cemetery otherwise."

Eden blinked, confused. "The park?" Understanding dawned on her face. She paled. "You mean, that night I camped out in my tent? Those noises I heard. That was you?!"

"Yes." He frowned. "It took me a whole damn day to find you after that. Good thing I did too."

Galliad drummed his fingers on the table, his expression stern. "Does anyone else know the staff is here, in this realm?"

Cedric could tell Galliad was still upset by this turn of events. After all, the mage was the one who had secured the Bloodcursed Devilwood Summoning Staff from the Nine Hells, centuries past.

"There are rumors circulating about its presence on Earth, yes. And our enemy is looking for it still." He paused. "I just made sure to sow enough false leads to keep them busy."

Galliad stared. "False leads?"

"Yes." A mirthless smile twisted Cedric's lips. "They think it's in a bank vault."

CHAPTER TWENTY-FOUR

"That's not Eden," Brianna said across the phone line.

Morgan frowned. "Are you sure?"

"I know my own daughter," Brianna replied, her tone adamant. "And that person is not her."

Morgan and Cassius studied the monitor in the back of the Argonaut van. Maggie had spotted someone who fit Eden's description on a recording from the security camera in the youth hostel, in Mission Dolores. They'd opted to view the video she'd sent with Brianna. Adrianne and Bailey hadn't uncovered anything that could help them track down the missing girl's whereabouts in Presidio Heights or the cemetery and this was their only lead so far.

The recording showed Eden Monroe returning to the hostel early that morning to retrieve her backpack. The previous day's video had her leaving the place in the afternoon. She was wearing the same clothes she'd gone out in and appeared calm and collected as she came out of the building with her bag at about 7 a.m.

"Maggie just forwarded another recording from a loan shop around the corner from the hostel," Adrianne said. "She thought it might be useful to see what direction Eden was headed in." She grimaced. "It's the only place in the immediate neighborhood that has a camera facing the road, so we'd be damn lucky if she took that route."

"Let's watch it anyway," Cassius said.

The screen filled with another view of the Mission Dolores neighborhood. Luck was on their side for once. Eden came into view a short while later. She headed down the street past the loan shop, paused under some trees at the next intersection, and looked around furtively before moving deeper into the shadows.

Morgan straightened. Eden's lips moved ever so slightly, as if she were murmuring an incantation. He frowned when the girl's eyes flashed emerald. Her figure shifted, her body growing taller and assuming a muscular, male frame while her hair shortened and darkened to a rich honey.

The guy who'd disguised himself as the missing girl vanished around the corner of a building.

"Well, I'll be damned," Bailey muttered.

Adrianne rewound the video and froze the frame.

"Anyone recognize that man?" Brianna said, her voice fraught with tension.

Morgan glanced around the van and clocked his

team's negatives. "No. We'll run his face through our database and see if we get any hits."

"I'll do the same at my end." Brianna paused. "Thank you for everything you're doing to find my daughter."

Morgan ended the call just as they arrived at their target destination. They split up as per their plan, Cassius taking Adrianne, Zach, and Charlie with him, while Morgan, Bailey, and Julia formed the secondary team. They took up positions and settled in for the wait.

"How confident is Charlie about this?" Julia murmured an hour later where she crouched behind Bailey's illusion shield.

"Pretty confident," Morgan replied. "You know what he's like."

"Overcautious and prone to underestimating himself?" Bailey said wryly.

"Exactly," Morgan grunted. "Which means he had to be damn certain for him to even suggest this."

"Well, let's hope these guys bite and I don't end up spending the night here with you two for nothing," Julia said.

Bailey grinned. "I know whom Morgan would rather be spending the night with."

Morgan narrowed his eyes at the wizard.

"You know I can hear you, right?" Cassius grumbled over their comm line.

It was past midnight before Charlie's predictions about the bank robbers' next move proved to be correct. A shift in the air currents in the subway tunnel brought a whisper of voices. Morgan tensed, his preternatural gaze piercing the shadows.

"Here they come," Bailey murmured.

Eight figures emerged from the gloom. They were dressed in black and had masks covering their lower faces. Morgan caught a flurry of faint scents. He frowned.

So, they have sorcerers and an enchanter. They must be good to have left no trace of their presence at the crime scenes.

Though he was nowhere near as capable as Cassius at picking up the distinctive smell of someone's soul core, he was getting better at it. He guessed sticking close to the Empyreal had something to do with that, as well as his recently awakened powers.

After analyzing the Altered Mind box for two days and visiting the locations of all the robberies, Charlie had deduced that the bank robbers would return to the scene of their latest crime to retrieve it.

"It's too valuable a device for them to abandon," the enchanter had told them. "The reason they left it on site was to confuse the cops. There was a secondary enchantment that kicked in after the first one. It was weaker but its intention was all too clear. It was meant to focus the investigators' attention in the wrong direction."

"So, you're saying they deliberately abandoned their most valuable asset on site and risked its discovery, all for the sake of fooling San Francisco PD?" Adrianne had said skeptically.

"I know it seems far-fetched when you say it like

that, but they were confident their ruse would work," Charlie had replied.

"Man, those guys really don't want us to get involved in their business, do they?" Zach had murmured.

Morgan had asked Lambert and Willis to get them the security camera feeds from the banks that had been hit the week that followed the initial robberies. To Charlie's complete lack of surprise, the recordings five days after the break-ins had been wiped clean.

No one outside their team, Strickland, and the two San Francisco PD detectives working the case knew they'd discovered the Altered Mind box and the secret tunnels the robbers had dug to reach the bank vaults. Cassius had insisted they keep the information under wraps, just in case it proved to be useful for setting a trap.

Looks like his instincts were right on target. It's a good thing we put everything back the way we found it after Charlie told us his conclusions this morning.

They hadn't been able to pinpoint exactly where the robbers would enter the subway system. Cassius and Charlie had estimated it to be anywhere within a half-mile radius of the bank. They waited until the figures disappeared inside the hidden passage before heading after them. A faint vibration came from Bailey's cell phone when they emerged into the basement under the bank. He glanced at the screen.

"It's Maggie. Cameras in the building just went offline. The tech team are trying to trace where the command came from."

"Good," Morgan muttered.

They were halfway up the security stairs leading to the first floor when the sound of a muffled explosion reached their ears. They broke into a run.

"Looks like they started the party without us!" Julia said grimly.

Morgan took point as they approached the main hall, his pulse accelerating. Light flared in the shadows ahead as Cassius and the others engaged the bank robbers who'd come to retrieve the Altered Mind box. Three figures guarded the end of the corridor, their silhouettes stark against the bright flashes of magic. They whirled around when they heard Morgan's footsteps.

Bailey shielded them from the spell bombs they cast their way. This gave Morgan and Julia more than enough time to reach their attackers, their wings unfurling as they bolted toward the enemy.

Metal clanged as Morgan's sword met a sorcerer's dagger. The man yelped, the Stark Steel edge catching the side of his hand. He pulled back and muttered an incantation, a heavy frown furrowing his brow. Morgan stiffened, watching spheres of crimson light burst into life next to the man's shoulders. He recognized the acrid scent instantly.

That's bloodcursed magic! But—how?!

CHAPTER TWENTY-FIVE

The sorcerer thrust his hands out and hurled the spheres at Morgan. He swore and blocked the attack with his wings, magic sparking hotly across his feathers.

The second sorcerer was holding his own against Julia a short distance away, knife scraping along her blade. Bailey gritted his teeth where he stood behind them, the defensive shield he'd erected sparking and wavering under the third figure's attack. The woman easily deflected the spell bombs the wizard lobbed at her, her dark eyes mocking above her mask.

She snatched a wand from her waist and unleashed the staff within, arcane symbols flashing on the wood as she used it to focus her magic. The sorcerers retreated to her side.

Morgan narrowed his eyes. *A mage?!*

The spell bomb she launched blasted Morgan and Julia into the wall and drew shocked grunts from them both. Cracks raced along the floor and up the walls of the hallway. Morgan sat up and shook his head dazedly.

"Shit!" Julia cursed next to him. "They're strong!"

Morgan scowled. The fact that the mage could conceal her scent so well could only mean one thing.

She was a Level One magic user.

The woman widened her stance and slammed her staff into the ground. The red light of bloodcursed magic filled the corridor. Alarm shot through Morgan. He moved, black wind bursting into life around him.

He reached Bailey in time to fend off the attack, his Demigod powers sending the deadly explosion toward the ceiling. Debris rained down upon them as concrete and plaster gave way, the beams forming the structure of the building glowing crimson where they lay exposed, metal fractured and distorted under the woman's magic.

"You okay?" Morgan growled as he lowered his black wings, inky currents swirling around his feathers.

Bailey nodded, face pale. "Yeah."

Julia raised her hands and clenched her fists, light dancing under her skin as she drew on her Terrene powers. The floor under the mage and her companions erupted violently upward, sending them into the air. A translucent red globe shivered into existence around the three figures, stopping them short of crashing into the ceiling. The bubble drifted to the ground, the magic users levitating within it.

Morgan's stomach clenched. Though he wasn't picking up the stench of black magic from their attackers, the barrier protecting the mage and the two sorcerers reminded him eerily of the incident with Chester Moran a month ago, in the alley behind *Occulta*. He exchanged a guarded glance with Julia and Bailey and saw the same disquiet reflected in their eyes.

Morgan unleashed his sword of dark wind, the weapon throbbing with his new powers. He shot up in the air and dropped toward the sphere in an arc, a harsh sound leaving him as he brought both blades down.

The impact sent vibrations up his arms. The barrier warped but held.

Morgan raised his swords again. Heat flared in his soul core, making him blink. He sensed Cassius's powers swell across their bond. Dazzling brilliance bathed the corridor as the Empyreal appeared from the direction of the main hall, Heaven's Light wrapped around his body and his Stark Steel blade, his wings white and his eyes bright with seraphic energy. A frown marred his face at the sight of the mage and the two sorcerers inside the barrier.

He met Morgan's gaze. *"Together."*

They moved as one. A violent detonation shook the corridor and rattled the building as their weapons crashed into the bloodcursed sphere. A thin crack appeared in the shield. The mage glowered at them from behind the barrier, her gaze full of loathing. The symbols on her staff flared bright with magic.

A high-pitched noise exploded in the passage, making Morgan wince.

Cassius's eyes widened. *"Take cover!"*

Morgan darted back and dropped down in front of Julia and Bailey. He spread his wings in time to shield them, the violent gusts from the blast forcing his feet across the ground. Julia and Bailey scowled, the angel and the wizard wielding their own powers to protect him as best they could from debris and magic.

The pressure waves finally abated. Deafening silence descended in the wake of the explosion. Morgan twisted around, chest tight with apprehension.

The mage and the sorcerers had vanished, along with the bloodcursed magic protecting them.

Cassius landed next to them.

"Are you okay?" he asked anxiously.

The radiance bathing him faded, his feathers darkening to black and red once more.

"Yeah. You?"

Cassius breathed a sigh of relief. "I'm good. We should—"

He gasped, the rest of his words swallowed by Morgan's mouth as Morgan pulled him into his arms.

Adrianne's voice rose from the direction of the main hall.

"Where the heck did those guys go?" the sorceress complained as she came into view. She stopped and scowled when she saw Morgan and Cassius kissing. "For Pete's sake you two, we're still on the job!"

Julia sighed, her Stark Steel blade shrinking back down to a knife.

Morgan reluctantly let go of Cassius. The telltale color staining the Empyreal's cheeks indicated he'd enjoyed the kiss as much as Morgan had.

"You really need to stop doing that," he mumbled.

Zach and Charlie appeared behind Adrianne, their clothes and hair mildly singed.

Bailey stared at the spot where the mage and the sorcerers had disappeared. "Any idea what just happened? Those guys were using bloodcursed magic. How that's even possible?"

"It wasn't their magic." Cassius frowned. "That bloodcursed energy belonged to that mage. She shared her powers with them."

Charlie was holding the Altered Mind box in his hands, a frown on his face. "Those guys space-jumped out of here."

"Space-jumped?" Bailey grimaced. "Is that new lingo for 'used a portal?'"

"Kinda. It's faster than a standard portal and difficult to track," the enchanter muttered. "They must have used that mage's bloodcursed magic to do it."

"You alright?" Julia arched an eyebrow. "You look like you're about to bite someone."

Charlie hesitated. "I think one of their sorcerers is playing them."

Morgan stared, his surprise reflected on Cassius and the others' faces.

"Why do you say that?" Cassius asked.

"Because he got his hands on the device but didn't take it. Instead, he gave me this."

Charlie unfisted his hand. A rectangular object sat

in his palm. It was a black matchbox with the word *Ohomgath* written in red across it.

Morgan frowned.

Ohomgath was the name of one of Bostrof Orzkal's fight clubs, the Lucifugous demon who used to rule the Shadow Empire.

CHAPTER TWENTY-SIX

EDEN WOKE UP FROM A FITFUL SLEEP, HER THROAT parched. The blanket covering her slid to her waist as she slowly sat up, her vision adjusting to the gloom.

Cedric lay on a couch a few feet away, his chest moving slowly with his breaths.

They were in Galliad's apartment, above his shop in Chinatown. The place was more pleasant than Eden had thought it would be, the Dryad's choice of furnishings giving it a warm, cozy feel. Cedric had refused Galliad's offer for one of them to take his bedroom, saying they couldn't possibly do that to an old man.

Eden had watched their dry exchange with a trace of envy. Though Cedric and Galliad had different views on certain matters, it was clear they were friends and respected one another.

Galliad had insisted they stay with him until they got to the bottom of why the ghouls were after Eden. Cedric had agreed. As for the people seeking the

Bloodcursed Devilwood Summoning Staff, Galliad had already started working on a list of potential suspects.

Eden moved carefully off the couch and tip-toed past Cedric. She got a glass of water from the kitchen and gazed out of the window overlooking Grant Avenue. The street was still busy despite the late hour, people milling along the sidewalks under a light, autumnal shower.

There was a magic market somewhere underneath Chinatown. Eden had never been to it. She wondered if she would have the opportunity to visit it one day.

A faint glow caught her eye as she made her way back to the lounge. The door to Galliad's study was ajar, wavering yellow light seeping under the frame and through the slit-like opening. She slowed and hesitated before approaching it. The door swung on silent hinges when she pushed it a few inches.

Galliad sat reading at his desk. He looked up and smiled.

"Come on in."

"I'm sorry, I didn't mean to disturb you."

"You're not." He indicated the armchair opposite him. "Take a seat."

Eden padded quietly over to the chair. She sat down and drew her knees to her chest, the fire in the hearth warming her exposed skin.

Galliad closed his book. "Can't sleep?"

Eden noted the tome's ornate cover and gilded page edges. "It's a bit hard to do that when there are monsters after you."

Galliad leaned back in his chair, his expression

pensive. "Cedric was somewhat frugal with the facts when I asked him who you were and how you two met." He arched an inquisitive eyebrow, his blue eyes bright. "Care to enlighten me?"

Eden chewed her lip. *I guess there's no harm telling him about Brianna and Hexa.*

Galliad listened wordlessly while she spoke falteringly about her mother, the guild of magic users, and her desperate plan to escape their clutches. Admiration danced across his face when she described how she'd run away from home and stayed in a park that first night, before heading for the youth hostel she'd intended to hide at ahead of her trip to San Diego.

"And then Cedric found me," she finished quietly.

She could tell from Galliad's expression that Cedric had told him what had gone down in the grounds of the church, in Mission Dolores.

"How do you feel about your mother and Hexa now that you know what they did?" he said after she'd fallen silent. "Do you resent her still?"

Brianna's face swam before Eden. Her chest grew tight.

"I...don't know. On a purely practical level, I can understand why she did what she did. But," she frowned, "I think I would rather have had my mother's love and a short life, than one where I wished I'd never been born."

Galliad's eyes grew distant. "The love of a parent for her child is unfathomable. And no parent wants to see their child die before them. Remember that, when you next see your mother."

Eden pondered whether that chance would ever come. She'd been adamant when she'd run away from home that she never wanted to see Brianna again for the rest of her life. But now, a strange longing stirred inside her. She had so many questions she wanted to ask her mother.

"If our paths were to cross again, I—"

Light flared on Galliad's arm, halting her words. Eden stared at the bracelet on his wrist. She hadn't noticed it before.

It was identical to Cedric's.

Galliad stiffened and rose to his feet. Rapid footsteps sounded outside the study.

Cedric stormed inside the room, his laurel staff in hand. "They're close!"

He lobbed Eden's shoes across the room.

She caught them with a fumble and put them on hastily before standing up, her belly twisting with alarm. "Who's close?"

"The ghouls. They've tracked us down." Cedric clenched his jaw. "Shit! I shouldn't have used my magic on that punk!"

"What's done is done, Your Highness," Galliad said in a steely voice. "Let's get you two out of here."

He shoved the book he'd been reading inside his kaftan and removed a wand from behind his back. It transformed into an elmwood staff, symbols flaring into life along the rough surface. Warmth bloomed in Eden's belly, her magic responding to the Dryad's.

They were halfway down the hall leading to the front door when a crash came from somewhere below them.

"Damn it, they're in the shop!" Galliad whirled around. "The fire escape! Quickly!"

They followed him into the kitchen.

Galliad pushed the sash window open, climbed out, and offered his hand to Eden. "Be careful. It's slippery."

Goosebumps erupted on Eden's exposed arms as she stepped onto the metal landing. A chilly wind was blowing across the city, bringing the taste of winter with it. They headed rapidly down the fire escape.

The metal frame vibrated violently under Eden's feet as they neared the ground. She looked up and saw two ghouls climb over the windowsill of Galliad's kitchen. More appeared from the mouth of the alleyway leading to the shop, the stench of rotting meat heralding their arrival. Crimson eyes focused on her, sending a shiver down her spine.

"Come! We can't fight them here!" Galliad vaulted over the railing and landed smoothly on the ground. "We have to get them away from these people!"

Eden and Cedric took the final steps at a run and followed him as he raced down the street. The ghouls gave chase, their shrieks ringing in Eden's ears. Alarmed cries rose along the avenue when people registered the monsters' presence.

Galliad took the corner of the next block without slowing. Eden tried to do the same and gasped when she slid on the wet sidewalk. She would have fallen had Cedric not grabbed her wrist. Heat rushed up her arm and flared inside her soul core. The bloodcursed pendant shimmered into view, crimson light dancing on the wood.

It pulsed with Eden's every heartbeat.

"Damn it!" Cedric cursed. "Now they'll be able to track us down wherever we go!"

Galliad glanced over his shoulder, a frown furrowing his brow.

"Sorry!" Eden mumbled.

"It's not your fault," Cedric said grimly, his fingers tightening around hers as they bolted between the people crowding the street. "None of this is!"

They took another corner, darted into an alley, and came out onto a busy road. Galliad headed swiftly south.

"Down here!" he ordered a moment later.

He made for a shadowy opening on their left. Darkness swallowed them as they started down a flight of stone steps.

Eden's breaths came hard and fast where she kept pace with Cedric, his hand clasped tightly around hers still. Her vision was strangely clear.

Is it my magic?!

She had little time to wonder more. They reached the bottom of the stairs and bolted after Galliad as he dashed into a tunnel lit by flame torches, their shadows dancing erratically on the rock walls. A low drone rose in the distance. It became a chaotic din as they approached the end of the passage. They emerged into a giant underground space bathed in the orange glow of hundreds of flame torches.

Eden had but seconds to process the sights and

sounds around her before Cedric tugged on her arm and dragged her after Galliad. Her heart pounded in her chest as they darted past colorful stalls and shop fronts, the smells of the exotic goods on display washing over her in tantalizing waves.

This must be the magic market!

A scream tore the air behind them. More followed.

Eden glanced over her shoulder and caught a glimpse of the ghouls as they leapt and bounded across the roofs of tents and stands. The monsters were catching up to them fast.

They turned a corner and dashed down another alleyway. It widened after some two hundred feet. The area ahead opened up. They came out into a flagstone square with a water fountain.

"Get out of here!" Galliad shouted at the crowd packing the place.

Magic flared in his hand as he ran toward the center, a dazzling green sphere that spun and shimmered. He cast it above the heads of the people turning to look at him with puzzled expressions. Eden gasped as the ball exploded. The crowd scattered amidst shocked cries.

Galliad stopped next to the water fountain, Eden and Cedric seconds behind. "We'll make our stand here! Get ready, Your Highness!"

They took up position, Eden behind them.

Panic became terror when people saw the approaching ghouls, the monsters' grotesque forms rendered even more eerie by the light from the flame torches. The last stragglers streamed past them, faces ashen as they sought cover in nearby alleys.

The ghouls landed in the square with thuds that shook the ground. Blood dripped down the chins of two of the monsters, bits of flesh and gore dangling from their fangs. One of them held a head in its claws, like some kind of gory basketball.

Eden pressed a hand to her mouth and retched.

"Now!" Galliad shouted.

He and Cedric slammed their staffs onto the ground. Green light exploded from the weapons and filled the air. It condensed into a glowing barrier some twenty feet wide around them. The ghouls screeched and launched themselves at the wall.

"How long will it hold?" Cedric said grimly.

"Against ordinary ghouls? Forever." Galliad frowned. "But these ghouls aren't ordinary."

Cedric swore. "So, I was right! I thought I sensed something strange about them when I fought them back at the cemetery!"

Eden stared at them, her heart in her mouth. "What do you mean?"

"These creatures have bloodcursed magic in them." Galliad glanced at her. "It's not as powerful as yours." His expression hardened. "But it means they are resilient little bastards that could very well get through our shields if we're not careful."

The barrier shivered as the ghouls slammed into it repeatedly.

Eden's nails sank into her palms, fear forming a leaden weight in the pit of her stomach.

CHAPTER TWENTY-SEVEN

Cassius studied the exquisite porcelain teapot the demon held in his large hands, somewhat bemused. "Sure."

They were in the Lucifugous's office, in *Ohomgath*. It was but one of several such fight clubs scattered across the city. A monitor on the wall showcased the match currently taking place in the main ring between Bostrof's champion, Crusher, and another demon.

Morgan cocked a thumb at the mini bar. "What happened to whiskey?"

Bostrof sighed as he poured Cassius a steaming cup of dark tea. "Lilaia says I need to lose some weight, so I'm abstaining from alcohol for a month."

Julia and Adrianne exchanged an amused glance. Zach smiled.

"You're just another henpecked husband, huh?" Bailey muttered.

Cassius accepted the drink Bostrof proffered. The

demon was all muscle and sinew. He doubted he would ever get love handles. A smile tugged at his lips while he put milk and sugar in his tea.

I bet she just wanted him not to drink for a while.

Whereas it would have taken them some time to track down the evasive Lucifugous king's whereabouts in the past, the events involving Chester Moran meant they now had a direct line to Bostrof.

The demon took the seat opposite them. "Anyway, to what do I owe the pleasure of you and your team's visit?"

Cassius and Morgan looked over at Charlie. The enchanter came forward and put the matchbox on the coffee table.

"This is one of yours, right?" Cassius asked Bostrof.

The demon dipped his chin. "Sure looks like it."

Morgan propped his elbows on his knees. "Care to tell us why a sorcerer suspected of being a member of the group who's been breaking into the city's banks for the past two weeks handed this to Charlie tonight?"

Bostrof grew still. A frown marred his brow. "You're involved in that case?"

Cassius exchanged a guarded look with Morgan. "Yes. The detectives running the investigation approached Argonaut for help, with the blessing of their Deputy Chief and Strickland. The husband of their police commander detected magic on his wife when she returned home from one of the crime scenes, so the case falls within our jurisdiction."

"We've since confirmed that the perpetrators are magic users who utilized a device called an Altered

Mind box and an explosive made from Lightning Flash to carry out their robberies," Morgan said gruffly. "They left the box at the last bank they ransacked. Charlie thought they would return to retrieve it a few days later. He was right."

"There's more," Cassius added. "We encountered a bloodcursed magic user tonight. A female mage who was part of the group who turned up at the bank with an enchanter and some sorcerers. She is strong. Real strong." He faltered. "As strong as Chester was when Morgan and I fought him under the cathedral."

"I can attest to that," Julia said in a hard voice.

Bostrof studied them with a troubled expression. "Bloodcursed magic? You're certain of this?"

"Yes," Cassius replied. "As improbable as it sounds, the mage we crossed paths with possesses a bloodcursed soul core and is able to control its power. She's also able to gift her magic to her acolytes."

"That mage goes by the name of Rebecca," Bostrof said after a short silence. "I'm certain it's not her real name. She's part of an organization I've been investigating for a while. One that has infiltrated the underworld of our city and many others on the west coast without the main players even realizing it. No one knows much about them and those who have tried to find out have all died. There are rumors circulating that they use ghouls to do their dirty work."

Surprise jolted Cassius. "Ghouls?"

"Yes."

"You got a name for that organization?" Morgan asked.

Bostrof drummed his fingers on his knee. "They call themselves *Ouroboros*. I only discovered this after I successfully seeded a spy in the group."

Julia arched an eyebrow. "The sorcerer who gave us that matchbox?"

Bostrof nodded. "Yes. They don't fully trust Karl yet. In fact, from what he's observed, they don't really trust any of their members. If they have a base, they haven't shared its location with him. The one who contacts them and gives them their orders is Rebecca. But Karl is pretty confident she answers to someone else."

"Why would an organization name themselves after a phallic symbol?" Bailey muttered. This earned him a battery of stares. He shrugged. "I'm just saying."

Cassius frowned. "*Ouroboros* stands for more than just a fertility symbol. It also signifies the cycle of life, death, and rebirth."

Unease stirred inside him once more. He couldn't help but think of the man who had possessed Chester in their final battle. The one whom the Demigod he had once been had told him was Death.

Is this connected to Chester's master, like I feared?

The vague suspicion he'd had when he'd fought the female mage danced at the back of his mind.

"Has your spy told you what they're after?" Morgan said.

"No," Bostrof replied. "Most of *Ouroboros* have no idea what they're looking for. Rebecca is probably the only one who does. But my gut feeling tells me that, whatever it is, it's unique and dangerous."

"We think it's a magical artifact," Cassius said.

Disquiet filled Bostrof's face. "You mean, like the Eternity Key?"

Cassius hesitated. "Yes."

"We've been looking for a guy called Usman Abbas," Morgan said. "He's a drug dealer who recently handled a large shipment from the Astrea Sea, probably the Lightning Flash *Ouroboros* has been using. He might know the location of their hideout if they have one."

Bostrof grimaced. "He doesn't."

Cassius shared a startled look with the others. "You know where Abbas is?"

"Yes. He's currently in a cell fifty feet under us," the demon grumbled. "I was intending to send him to the Astrea Sea with a few of my agents to look for his source. But that might not be necessary anymore."

"You mentioned ghouls," Adrianne said. "We're currently trying to find a missing girl who was attacked by a pack of them. Her name is Eden Monroe. She's Brianna Monroe's daughter."

Surprise widened Bostrof's eyes. "What?"

"That's not the only thing Eden Monroe has in common with *Ouroboros*," Cassius said. "Her soul core is bloodcursed."

"Brianna and a group of Hexa mages bound Eden's soul at birth," Morgan explained at Bostrof's stunned expression. "It's the only reason the kid's made it to her teens without self-imploding."

"I'm beginning to think these two cases are linked," Cassius said thoughtfully.

The others stared at him.

He shrugged. "Bloodcursed magic is a once-in-a-century event. To have two incidents involving it in the same city at the same time cannot be a coincidence."

"I think you're right," Morgan muttered.

Adrianne narrowed her eyes. "In which case, Eden is in a lot more danger than we originally thought."

An urgent knock came at the door. Bostrof glanced at the feed from the security camera outside the office.

He frowned. "Come in."

One of his men stormed through the door, expression agitated. "Sorry to disturb you, boss! I thought you'd want to know. Something's happening in the magic market, in Chinatown!"

Bostrof raised an eyebrow. "What kind of thing?"

"An attack of some sort. One of your tenants just called. He said a few people are dead and several of your shops are damaged. He was rambling about ghouls and a couple of mages. There's a girl with them."

Cassius's pulse spiked. He shared an alarmed glance with the others.

Could it be—?!

"Eden," Morgan said grimly.

They rose and headed briskly for the exit.

"Wait," Bostrof said in a hard voice. "It'll be faster through the sewers."

CHAPTER TWENTY-EIGHT

CEDRIC KICKED A GHOUL IN THE GUT, SWIPED THE LEGS out from under another, and narrowly missed the claws aimed at his face.

Shit! There's no end to them!

Their barrier had lasted exactly twelve minutes. They had immediately erected a smaller, stronger shield around Eden while they engaged the ghouls. More of the monsters were pouring into the market, the cursed magic inside the girl and the pendant on his bracelet a lure they seemed unable to resist.

The Bloodcursed Devilwood Summoning Staff shimmered in and out of sight as he fought the creatures, the weapon straining to get to the one it knew could wield it. An explosion ripped the square behind him. Cedric blocked a strike to his flank and glanced over his shoulder.

Galliad's eyes and skin were aglow with the magic of their kind. The air shimmered emerald on a pressure wave that sent four ghouls slamming into the stalls on the west side of the square. Leaves and twigs sprouted in the mage's hair and flesh as he retraced his steps toward the monsters trying to rip through the barrier around Eden, his Dryad powers coming through in formidable pulses, the flagstone floor cracking under his steps.

Cedric clenched his jaw. Dryads did not like to display the full extent of their abilities in other realms, unless they were at war or their lives were in peril.

Well, I guess this situation satisfies both conditions!

He deflected another flurry of attacks, took a deep breath, and focused on the magic throbbing in his soul core. Arcane symbols flashed green on his laurel staff. The weapon thickened and lengthened, amplifying his powers even as it doubled in strength. Shoots appeared on his skin, the buds blooming into leaves that shimmered with Dryad magic. A blackthorn and alderwood crown formed on his head, the mark of his royal lineage.

Cedric moved through the ghouls like wind across a field, his steps swift and certain, his attacks precise and deadly. The monsters' screams cut off abruptly as the laurel staff smashed into their jaws and windpipes with lightning-fast strikes. Their knees buckled under his powerful kicks, bones snapping with sharp cracks. Blood flicked onto his face and hair and soaked into his clothes as he stormed through the creatures, evading their fangs and claws by a whisper. Still, more came, their numbers legion. The square soon filled with dark bodies and crimson eyes.

A harsh grunt reached him. He looked over to the source of the sound and stiffened.

Galliad had disappeared under a pile of ghouls. Flashes of magic escaped through gaps between the monsters' tightly packed bodies as the mage fought to break free. The air shivered with a sudden burst of energy. Goosebumps rose on Cedric's skin.

Green radiance exploded in the center of the square. He grunted and dug his feet into the ground as the ripples washed over him, his mage magic thumping in tempo with Galliad's.

The monsters rose on an upward wave, their screeches piercing. Galliad straightened from where he'd been crouching, his dreadlocks flutteringly with savage waves of power as they floated around his head, his expression one of fury. Water left the fountain behind him in thin, spiraling jets that got absorbed by his body. More shoots mushroomed on his body, thickening his limbs.

The spell bombs he cast finished the ghouls before they crashed onto the ground.

Cedric caught a flicker of movement out of the corner of his eye. He jumped back and narrowly avoided the knife that cut through the space where he'd been standing. The weapon slowed and swiveled around in mid-air before coming at him at a dizzying speed. His eyes widened.

What the—?!

Cedric moved. To his shock, the blade reached him, cutting a thin line in his cheek and drawing a gasp from his lips. The weapon smacked handle first into the palm of a dark-clad figure some thirty feet away. The man's eyes mocked him above his mask as he advanced toward him. Cedric gritted his teeth, clocking the other similarly dressed figures appearing around the square.

Who the hell are these assholes?!

Galliad had registered the newcomers' arrival. He moved closer to the barrier shielding Eden, his face grim.

Cedric's knuckles whitened on his staff. The ghouls they could have managed. The black-clad magic users were something else. He could smell a foul scent coming from their soul cores. For some unfathomable reason, their powers were tainted with bloodcursed magic.

Damn it! We're outnumbered!

"Your Highness, do you remember what I said when I left our kingdom?" Galliad called out to him.

Cedric met the mage's gaze. "You vowed to always protect our people and our court."

"My promise still stands." Roots sprouted from Galliad's legs, anchoring him to the ground. "Once you see an opportunity, take Eden and run. The two of you must not fall into these people's hands. I will shield you with my life if I have to."

Cedric swallowed, the truth in the mage's words resonating inside him. He had grown up hearing tales of Galliad's legendary adventures in other realms and the numerous times he'd danced close to death in the midst of battle. A faint smile tugged at his lips despite their dire circumstances.

"You realize your wife will have my hide if you die because of me, right?"

Galliad chuckled. "She does have a temper, but even I don't think she'd dare raise a hand against the royal family." His expression sobered. "Get ready, Your Highness."

The air thickened, growing warm with magic. Emerald light flooded the square as the Dryad's powers expanded. The flagstone floor trembled.

The sorcerers halted in their tracks where they'd been converging on the mage, expressions wary. Cedric's gaze found Eden. She stood frozen inside the barrier, her face ashen with fear. He opened his mouth to call out to her.

Crimson light detonated above the square, all the more forbidding for being silent. The shockwave knocked the air out of his lungs and sent him tumbling to the ground. He grunted and rolled onto his hands and feet, body braced against the powerful gusts blowing across the market.

The wind faded. The brightness receded, only to be replaced by red-tinged shadows that obscured the light from the flame torches. Cedric rose unsteadily to his feet. His stomach twisted as he looked over to where Galliad and Eden stood.

An ethereal globe of sickening, bloodcursed magic pulsed and throbbed above them. A woman levitated inside the translucent sphere, her shrewd eyes observing them carefully above her mask. She dropped to the center of the square, the barrier surrounding her evaporating into a thin, red mist.

Flagstones exploded under her feet when she landed.

Galliad and Eden stumbled.

The woman straightened. "And here I thought tonight's little outing was a lost cause after those Argonaut fools messed with my plans." She glanced at the ghouls. "You have done well, my beasts. Why don't you go grab some of the humans hiding in the market and bring them here? You deserve a reward for your deeds."

Cedric scowled. Galliad narrowed his eyes.

The ghouls threw their heads to the skies and howled, the frenzied excitement of the impending hunt evident in the way their eyes flashed and their limbs twitched. A group of them exited the square at a loping run. Screams shattered the air a moment later.

"Now, mage." The woman advanced toward Galliad and Eden, power flaring crimson on her staff and under her every step. "Why don't you lower your barrier so I can get to Eden?"

Cedric startled. Eden's eyes widened.

"Don't look so shocked, girl," the woman drawled. "I've been waiting for this moment for a long time." Her gaze swiveled to Cedric. It grew slit-like when she saw the bracelet on his arm and the pendant dancing in and out of view. "And it seems you've found what we've been looking for." Her gaze flicked to the sorcerers next to Cedric. "Take him. But don't hurt him." Her tone turned condescending. "It seems we're dealing with royalty, after all. He'll make a good bargaining chip with the Dryad kingdom."

Cedric cursed and spun his laurel staff around his body, the weapon humming as it skimmed past the figures closing in on him.

"Like hell I'm going to let you touch him!" Galliad roared.

A trio of green spheres burst into existence above the mage's staff. He cast them at the woman. She deflected the attack with one hand and sent Galliad's spell bombs crashing into the stalls to her right. Debris rained over the square.

The woman's eyes flashed crimson. "My turn."

Galliad grunted. Cedric blinked.

The woman's fist had punched a hole in the Dryad's chest, her movement so fast they'd both missed it.

Shock flared on Galliad's face.

Fury burned through Cedric. *"Let him go, you bitch!"*

CHAPTER TWENTY-NINE

Horror widened Eden's eyes. The barrier around her flickered.

A vicious expression contorted the woman's face above her mask. She twisted her hand inside Galliad's body. Blood burst from the Dryad's lips.

"*No!*" Eden screamed.

"You fucking—!" Cedric growled.

A spell bomb exploded next to the prince's body. He gasped as another one detonated right in front of his face, dazzling him. Hands grabbed his arms. Magic restraints looped around his body, immobilizing him even as he struggled violently against the bonds. A sorcerer kicked the backs of his knees and sent him toppling to the ground. He landed on his side with a thud, his head striking the flagstone with a sickening sound.

"*Stop it!*" Eden yelled, her nails digging into her palms.

She could feel something building inside her. A

pressure she had never experienced before. Something was struggling to escape her body. Her gaze swung from the sorcerers who'd surrounded Cedric to the woman with her hand still buried in Galliad, anguish and rage storming through her in equal measure.

Galliad's shield vanished. The Dryad sagged, his grip limp on his staff.

Eden's breath froze on her lips. *No! This can't be happening! Cedric said Galliad was the strongest mage in his kingdom! He can't just—*

A low chuckle sounded. Eden stared.

Galliad's shoulders were shaking.

The woman narrowed her eyes. She cursed and jumped back in the next instant, a knot of branches wrapped around her fist. She blasted them away with a flash of red magic, cutting off the bough extending from Galliad's body.

The Dryad straightened, the branch retracting and twigs and leaves interlacing over his wound, his gaze emerald with power.

"I've fought creatures from the Nine Hells," he said in a hard voice. "If you think this little demonstration is going to kill me, you have another thing coming, hag!"

Cedric smiled fiercely.

The woman's eyes turned ugly. She glanced at the sorcerers next to him. "Why don't one of you take out the prince's left eye?"

Fury darkened Galliad's gaze. The woman blocked the spell bombs he cast at the sorcerers around Cedric with a red shield. Fear swamped Eden as a sorcerer grasped his knife and knelt by the Dryad prince. Two men grabbed his shoulders and held him flat on his back. Cedric cursed and struggled as the sorcerer with the knife pried his eye wide open.

Horror drenched Eden in a cold sweat. Time slowed.

No!

The denial echoed inside her, fierce and full of wrath. Her belly clenched on a wave of heat that drew a gasp from her throat. The command came to her, unbidden.

She knew what she had to do.

"*Come to me!*" Eden yelled, extending a hand toward Cedric.

The devilwood pendant materialized fully where it was attached to his bracelet, its surface shimmering with a red light. It ripped from the spell holding it prisoner, punched a hole through the hand of the sorcerer with his knife poised above Cedric's face, and flashed toward Eden. The sorcerer cried out and clutched his bleeding limb, his blade clattering harmlessly to the ground.

The female mage tried to grab the pendant as it sailed past her. The weapon twisted and avoided her grasp, the hum it made almost mocking. It slammed into Eden's hand with a sound that made the air tremble. Fire exploded up her arm and raced through her veins to the soul core beating deep inside her.

"Give that to me!" the woman snarled.

She headed for Eden. Galliad blocked her path.

It was all the time Eden needed. She took the

pendant and sliced a thin line in her palm with the sharp edge, her heart racing. Blood bloomed on her skin. It kissed the weapon and soaked into the wood. The medallion throbbed with a pulse of savage energy before transforming into a tall, dark staff swarming with arcane symbols. She stared.

The Bloodcursed Devilwood Summoning Staff!

The runes flashed crimson.

Eden gasped, power flooding her with a force that threatened to shatter her bones and tear her flesh asunder. Her consciousness flickered.

No! She gritted her teeth. *Stay awake, dammit!*

The staff responded to her will, slowing the flow of wild magic coursing through her blood, giving her body time to adapt. Eden focused on the pulsing source deep inside her and welcomed it all, her consciousness wavering ever so briefly before finally grasping onto the energy filling her every cell.

If it meant she could save Cedric and Galliad, she would gladly sell her soul to the devil right now.

A scarlet glow detonated around her, casting Galliad and the woman to the ground. Eden rose, bloodcursed magic oozing from her soul and seeping through her very pores.

***

Cedric's heart slammed against his ribs as he stared at Eden where she levitated some twenty feet above the ground.

A frown marred her brow and her eyes blazed

crimson as she glowered at the sorcerers and ghouls crowding the square, flashes of red light dancing on her hair as it floated around her head in slow, undulating waves. She seemed to have a measure of control over her magic this time, unlike the incident at the church.

Her gaze found the female mage.

The woman avoided the devastating spell bomb Eden cast at her by a hairbreadth.

Galliad cursed and erected a thick wall of thorns around himself and Cedric as the explosion tore through the square, blasting the fountain to pieces and ripping up the flagstones, the crimson pressure wave slicing several sorcerers and ghouls in half before it smashed into the frontage of the stalls and shops still standing.

The magic ropes binding Cedric loosened as the remaining sorcerers stumbled back in alarm. He grabbed his laurel staff and jumped to his feet.

A red sphere rose above the ruins of the square. The woman mage floated inside it, her face full of rage as she faced Eden.

"That weapon belongs to me, you ungrateful brat!" she roared.

"Oh, yeah?" Eden growled. "Well, come and get it, bitch!"

Cedric startled. *I've never heard her swear before!*

He blinked. The pressure inside the square was dropping.

The sinister magic that flooded the atmosphere in the next moment brought a flood of bile to the back of his throat. A scarlet haze swarmed the air. Cedric's eyes widened as a battery of crimson spheres flashed into existence in front of the woman mage.

"Let me show you what I can *really* do, little girl!"

She hurled the spell bombs at Eden.

Cedric moved, his legs shifting as if he were moving through sand, fear an icy prison clutching his heart. *"Eden!"*

Eden spun the bloodcursed staff. The weapon hummed, forming a shield that blocked the attack. She clenched her jaw as she was forced back half a dozen feet.

"Now!" the woman yelled.

Cedric froze.

Iron chains wreathed in magic shot up from the group of sorcerers who'd appeared below Eden, their presence masked by a veil of shadows until the very last moment. The shackles wound around her arms and legs and bit into her flesh, drawing blood. A cry of pain escaped her. Her eyes dimmed, the scarlet glow surrounding her fading.

The woman mage glared at the captive girl, her expression triumphant. "I've changed my mind. Kill the prince. I'll take care of the mage."

She moved toward Galliad, spell bombs forming on her palms.

Cedric gripped his laurel staff as a group of sorcerers converged on him once more, torn between running to Eden and protecting Galliad.

Shit! We could really do with some help right about—

Incandescent brightness filled the magic market.

Cedric sucked in air, black spots filling his vision. He squeezed his eyes shut and averted his head. Deafening silence descended around him. The radiance faded. He blinked and gazed at the center of the square, blood thrumming in his veins.

His breath locked in his throat.

An angel stood between the woman and Galliad, his dazzling white wings spread open to protect the Dryad. Lightning danced on his body and the sword he'd used to block the woman's bloodcursed magic attack.

"*You!*" she spat.

CHAPTER THIRTY

Divine power throbbed from Cassius as he scanned
the ruins of the square, dampening the effect of the
cursed magic saturating the air. He counted twenty
sorcerers and almost twice as many ghouls still
standing. Many more lay dead and bleeding, victims of
the fierce battle that had taken place before his arrival.
He spotted the young man who'd retrieved Eden's
backpack from the hostel standing a short distance to
his left.

Leaves and twigs covered the stranger's skin and
hair. A blackthorn and alderwood crown sat on his
head and the scent of juniper wafted from him as he
stood holding a laurel staff, his pupils gleaming green
with Dryad magic.

Admiration danced through Cassius. *They did a good
job holding off against so many of the enemy.*

The bloodcursed mage shot backward, a protective
sphere forming around her. Cassius studied the
woman thoughtfully.

Interesting. She's not escaping through a portal this time.

"That was good timing." The Dryad he'd shielded from the woman's deadly attack appeared beside him, eyes and skin aglow with magic. Only the faintest hint of juniper escaped his formidable soul core. His emerald gaze pierced Cassius. "It seems you are more than just an Empyreal, my friend."

Before Cassius could muster a reply, a violent whirlwind shot across the square.

Morgan smashed into the sorcerers wielding the chains binding Eden, strong gusts swirling around him. The men went flying into the facade of the shops at the edge of the square, the shackles in their hands clattering to the ground, their cries ending abruptly. His gray wings fluttered with his Aerial powers as he landed on the uneven flagstones.

"Hey, babe? Remember how I said we should stick together?" He leveled an accusing look at Cassius. "That is *not* what just happened."

The Dryad mage's amused gaze swung between them. "Babe?"

Cassius sighed. "Can you please focus? Those chains are made from black magic. Use your other sword to cut them."

"Okay," Morgan grumbled. "But this conversation is far from over."

The currents swirling around the Aerial turned jet black, as did his wings. A blade of pure darkness appeared in his left hand, power pulsing off it in strong waves.

The Dryad drew a sharp breath. "Oh my."

The female mage narrowed her eyes. "The Sword of Wind!"

Cassius and Morgan exchanged a surprised glance.

She knows the name of Morgan's weapon?

Morgan cut through the fetters holding Eden prisoner, his blade nullifying the black magic in the iron even as it carved through the metal. She gasped and fell, the staff in her hand shrinking to a tree-shaped, devilwood pendant.

He caught her before she hit the ground. "You okay, kid?"

Eden swallowed and nodded. "Put me down, please."

Her legs trembled as Morgan helped her to her feet. She glared at the female mage, her eyes fierce.

Cassius swallowed a smile, finally getting a good look at her. *She's Brianna's daughter, alright.*

Julia and Zach appeared to the west of the square, Adrianne, Bailey, and Charlie seconds behind. Bostrof joined them as they engaged the remaining ghouls and sorcerers.

The female mage rose inside her crimson bubble, her expression furious.

"I will take care of the angels!" she roared at her sorcerers. "Secure the girl and the staff!"

Bostrof's war cry echoed around the square as the enemy retreated from their fight and surged toward Morgan and Eden instead.

The symbols on the female mage's staff flared red.

Bloodcursed magic exploded across the market, so intense it rendered most of the people cowering in the nearby alleys unconscious. It wrapped around the sorcerers and ghouls, making their eyes glow red and amplifying their strength and speed. Cassius clenched his jaw at what he sensed behind the crimson haze swamping the air.

I was right. She's not just a mage!

"Be careful!" he shouted at Bostrof and the others as they charged toward the enemy. "Don't let their bloodcursed magic touch you!"

Morgan dropped a barrier of pure wind around Eden and took a defensive stance before her.

Seraphic energy flooded the square as Cassius unleashed his full powers. He sensed Morgan's surprise across their bonded soul cores. The Dryad mage staggered beside him but did not fall, the roots surrounding his legs sinking deeper into the ground. Lightning flared around Cassius. He knew without looking that his hair had brightened to pale gold. Armor materialized in the radiance bathing him, the Stark Steel plates fitting his trunk and limbs perfectly. His sword lengthened and broadened.

Cassius gripped the divine blade tightly, his unblinking gaze on the woman inside the red sphere. *"Morgan?"*

"Yeah?"

"She's a Demi."

The Dryad mage drew a sharp breath, understanding flaring on his face.

Morgan's eyes shrunk to slits. "So, *that's* why we couldn't defeat her back at the bank."

He slashed the heads of the three ghouls coming at

him clear off their torsos with a single swing of his Stark Steel sword and shot up from the ground, his black wings beating steadily. He moved, figure blurring. The bloodcursed mage grunted as he smashed into her barrier. She stretched out her hands and poured magic into the wavering shield.

She never saw Cassius move.

A shocked sound left her as he pierced her defenses from the side, his lightning-wreathed blade finding her right flank. Blood pooled around the wound and dripped down the Stark Steel sword.

Cassius frowned. The sphere did not shatter, like he'd thought it would.

The woman laughed when she registered his and Morgan's looks.

"*You fools!*" she hissed, her eyes flashing crimson. "You might be Demigods, like me, but I'm on a whole other level!" Her gaze swept the battlefield before finding Eden behind the wall of dancing black wind and the young Dryad who now guarded her. "Remember this, Eden. You and that staff *will* be mine. It is your curse and your fate. One your mother would have killed you to spare you from, had she known what the future held for her precious daughter!"

She vanished in a violent red flash, as did the sorcerers and the remaining ghouls.

"Damn it." Morgan scowled. "I wish we knew how they did that!"

Cassius stared at the empty space where the female mage had been, her words ringing in his ears and her blood congealing on his blade.

A HUSH FELL UPON THE SQUARE IN THE AFTERMATH OF their attackers' departure, the silence punctuated by the cries and moans of the people who'd been injured by the ghouls and falling debris.

Cedric whirled around, his crown and the shoots sprouting from his flesh shrinking as he retracted his Dryad powers. "Are you okay?!"

"Yes!" Eden answered.

The wind surrounding her abated. She stumbled into his arms, a shudder racing through her.

Cedric faltered for an instant before hugging her close. Bloodcursed magic throbbed between them as the pendant responded to his presence.

"It likes you," she mumbled.

He grimaced. "It does? Because all evidence points toward it being a major pain in my ass ever since I became its guardian."

She smiled against his chest despite the shivers racking her body. He pulled her closer, liking the beat of her heart against his.

"I finally get to meet the fabled Cassius Black," Galliad drawled.

"I don't know about fabled," the white angel muttered. "More like infamous."

The light bathing him faded as he resumed his human appearance, his hair shifting to a dark blond and his eyes turning gray. His blade transformed into a knife which he tucked at his back.

Cedric frowned as Cassius's wings vanished under

his clothes. He'd heard the angel's name plenty of times since he'd come to Earth. The Cursed Seraph. The Devil with the Black and Red Wings. The Angel of Misfortune. Those were but a few of the more palatable designations assigned to the seraph. He'd always suspected there was more to the story than that. Judging from Galliad's admiring look, he had been correct in his assumption.

The Aerial who'd accompanied Cassius was also back to his normal form. Cedric stared. There was something about the dark-haired angel that seemed oddly...familiar.

Galliad was also studying the man with an appraising look.

The Lucifugous demon joined them, along with the rag tag team of otherwordly and magic users who'd come to their rescue.

The Lucifugous gave the older Dryad a friendly slap on the back that almost sent him to his knees. "Galliad, my old friend. It has been some time since I've seen you in your full form."

"Hey, Bostrof," Galliad said with a wince. "Thanks for giving us a hand. And please, call me Brian." He patted his leaf-and-twig-strewn hair awkwardly, the greenery vanishing as he dampened his magic. "The circumstances unfortunately warranted my transformation."

"Wait." The blonde sorceress stopped and studied Galliad suspiciously. She muttered to herself while she counted on her fingers. "We're in Chinatown. You're a Dryad. And your name is Brian." Her eyes rounded. She gasped and pointed an accusing finger at the mage. "You're Lucy's source!"

"Oh." The Terrene angel with the Oriental features raised an eyebrow. "You're *that* Brian?"

"How is Miss Walters?" Galliad asked gallantly. "I haven't seen her in a while."

"She's still the bane of my life," the Aerial muttered.

Cassius rolled his eyes before looking over at Eden, his expression warming. "It's nice to finally meet you."

"You—" Eden stopped and swallowed, "—you know who I am?"

The angel smiled faintly. "Yes. Lois told me a lot about you."

Eden stiffened at his words.

Cassius's gaze shifted to Cedric. "Judging from the crown, you are Dryad royalty."

It wasn't so much a question as a statement.

Cedric met the angel's stare unflinchingly. "I am Cedric Esteban, the second prince of the Dryad kingdom." He dipped his head in a courteous bow. "Thank you for coming to our aid."

The others stared.

"Wow," the sorceress murmured. "Eden has good taste."

Eden flushed.

"Okay, who's going to say it?" The Terrene angel shrugged at their puzzled expressions. "I mean, I know we've just had a lot of information thrown at us, what with the Dryad planting roots in the middle of the magic market—"

She indicated Galliad.

Galliad looked down at the offshoots burgeoning from his feet. "Oh."

He retracted them, embarrassed.

"—to the royal over there and the girl with bloodcursed magic." The Terrene angel waved a hand at Cedric and Eden. She crossed her arms and arched an eyebrow at Cassius and the Aerial. "Is there something you two would like to tell us?"

"I have no idea what you're talking about," the Aerial said defensively.

"She means our Demigod status," Cassius murmured.

"Oh."

The Aerial made a face and rubbed the back of his neck.

"Er, April Fools?" he said in a fake jovial tone.

"It's October," the sorceress said flintily.

"I can't believe they withheld that kind of information from us," the dark-haired Aqueous demon murmured to the Terrene angel, his tone somewhat hurt.

"I know," the blond wizard grumbled. "We should ground them."

"Please," the enchanter muttered. "Coming from you, that sounds like you want to tie them up in some dungeon and do sexual stuff with them."

His friends gaped at him, Cassius included.

"What?" the enchanter snapped. "I'm having a shitty day, okay?"

"Just...who are you people?!" Eden mumbled.

CHAPTER THIRTY-ONE

BRIANNA STORMED INTO THE PRIVATE HOSPITAL ROOM, features ashen and blonde hair flying around her face. Malik and a woman Morgan didn't recognize followed a couple of steps behind her, their expressions equally distraught.

"Eden!" Brianna cried out.

"Mom," Eden whispered where she sat stiffly on the edge of the bed. She rose, hands trembling and eyes darkening with a storm of emotions.

Brianna dashed toward her. She rocked to an abrupt halt when she got within six feet of her daughter, her body lurching as she fought an inner battle.

"You can touch her," Cassius said quietly. "Her soul core is stable."

Brianna looked at him as if she'd seen a ghost. "What do you mean?!"

"Eden used a bloodcursed weapon tonight. It

stabilized her powers, somehow. And it gave her the ability to keep a rein on her soul core magic."

Brianna stared at Eden.

"Do you really mean that?" she whispered to Cassius. "I won't hurt her if I touch her?"

Sorrow filled Eden's face at the sight of her mother's deep-felt anguish.

"I doubt another mage could have managed what Eden did tonight without years of training." A sad smile tilted Cassius's lips. "Your daughter's a natural, Brianna."

Color brought a flush to Eden's pale cheeks at the compliment. Morgan had the feeling she rarely got praised. The girl gasped as Brianna closed the distance to her and hugged her fiercely.

Cedric shifted where he sat on a chair next to the bed, his expression awkward.

Morgan bit back a smile. *And that guy definitely doesn't do feelings.*

Malik narrowed his eyes accusingly at the Dryad prince. "Isn't that the man from the hostel?"

The woman beside him looked at him, surprised. "What hostel?" She glanced around the room, her expression growing apologetic. "I'm sorry, I haven't introduced myself. I'm Valerie Hartman, one of Brianna's aides."

"He is not your enemy," Galliad told Malik. The Dryad mage stood next to Cedric. "His Highness has saved young Eden's life on many an occasion now."

Malik blinked, startled. "His Highness?"

"Mom, I can't breathe!" Eden wheezed in Brianna's hold.

Brianna let her go with a contrite expression. "I'm sorry." She stood back and scanned her daughter anxiously from head to toe. "Are you okay? Did you get hurt?!"

Eden smiled weakly. "I'm alright. A medical mage put Blossom Silver on my wounds." She rolled up the sleeves of her shirt. "She said they won't leave a scar."

Tears glimmered in Brianna's eyes as she studied the livid marks the iron chains had left on Eden's skin. She folded her daughter carefully into her arms once more and pressed a tremulous kiss to her forehead. "I'm so sorry, baby. About everything. There's so much I need to tell you."

Eden squeezed her mother tightly, a low sob escaping her as she buried her face in her chest. "I have a lot to tell you too, mom."

A knock came at the door.

Strickland walked in without waiting for an answer. He paused when he saw them.

"Is this a bad time?" he said gruffly.

Morgan sighed. "Seeing as you look like you're about to commit murder, I suspect any time would be a bad time."

Strickland scowled. His gaze landed on Malik and Valerie. "We should keep this private."

Brianna dipped her chin at the sorcerer and the aide. They exited the room, Malik looking disgruntled. Tense silence fell in the wake of their departure.

Strickland crossed the floor to the window and looked out over the city, his expression tense. "The bureau is currently dealing with some hundred complaints regarding the incident at the magic market. San Francisco PD is already breathing down my neck about the victims who died there. Adrianne gave me a debrief when I was driving over here, but I still want to hear what happened from all of you." He turned and studied Galliad with a frown. "And you. I could have sworn I told you to lie low when you first came to my city."

The Dryad mage scratched his cheek, abashed. "I *was* lying low. But I couldn't exactly ignore His Highness when he came to me for help." He indicated Cedric. "Besides, this matter concerns all of us."

Strickland's gaze shifted to Cedric.

"I hope you have a valid reason as to why my agency wasn't made aware of your presence in my city...Your Highness," he said, his tone turning a fraction more respectful.

"Trust me, it's a good one," Cedric retorted grimly.

Strickland looked over at Brianna and Eden where they'd taken a seat on the edge of the bed.

"You have caused quite a ruckus, young lady," he told Eden sternly.

Eden chewed her lip, her expression forlorn.

Brianna bristled. "Francis, you need to back down. I won't have you—"

Strickland raised a conciliatory hand. "I'm not attacking your daughter, Brianna. I'm just stating facts. Now, how about you go first, Eden?"

Eden swallowed nervously as she became the center of attention.

Brianna clasped her fingers and patted them gently. "It's okay, sweetheart."

Cedric laid a comforting hand on Eden's knee. Brianna narrowed her eyes slightly.

Eden spoke haltingly at first. Her tone grew more confident as she described what had happened from the time she'd first spotted a ghoul to the night she'd run away from home. She talked of her plans to escape the city and how Cedric had saved her from the monsters in the park and the cemetery.

"That was the first time I…manifested my magic. A drop of my blood landed on the devilwood pendant attached to Cedric's bracelet when we were being attacked. I suspected that's what activated it, which is why I did the same thing at the magic market." She took the medallion out of her pocket and held it in her open palm. "It helped me defeat those creatures then and tonight."

Admiration darted through Morgan. He could tell the others were similarly impressed by Eden's swift deduction and action in the heat of battle.

She will make a powerful combatant.

"That pendant is what the bank robbers were after," Cassius told Strickland.

The Argonaut director frowned. "How do you know that?"

"Because the mage and sorcerers we laid a trap for tonight were the same ones who attacked these three in the magic market a few hours later." Morgan indicated

Eden and the two Dryads. "The female mage said they need both Eden and the pendant for whatever the hell it is they're planning to do."

Strickland stared at the medallion as if it were a bomb. "What the devil is that thing anyway?"

"That's the Bloodcursed Devilwood Summoning Staff," Galliad said.

CHAPTER THIRTY-TWO

Brianna startled. "What?" She and Strickland exchanged a shocked glance. "You mean, the legendary artifact the Dryads were rumored to be holding on to?!"

"Yes, the very same," the Dryad mage replied somberly. "Getting that thing out of the Nine Hells almost cost me my life, so you can imagine how I feel about seeing it roaming freely in your realm."

"It wasn't roaming freely," Cedric protested. "We bound it to my bracelet with a powerful spell."

"Yes, well, that *thing* has declared Eden its rightful owner and there's nothing we can do about it," Galliad grumbled.

Brianna paled. "Wait. What do you mean, the staff has claimed Eden as its rightful owner?!"

"They both have bloodcursed magic and it seems they match each other well." Galliad paused. "The staff wants Eden to be its mage."

Eden stared at the pendant, her expression dazed. "It—it chose *me?!*"

"Were you the one who put out those rumors about the staff being in a bank vault?" Cassius asked Cedric.

The Dryad prince made a face. "Yeah. Sorry about that. But it sure kept those assholes off my back for a while."

Morgan masked a grimace. *Lambert and Willis will be* pissed *if they find out about this.*

Strickland folded his arms across his chest, his face thunderous. "How about you tell us why you brought this weapon to Earth, Your Highness?"

Cedric looked tired all of a sudden. He blinked when Eden laid her hand over his. He took a deep breath and started talking.

The disquiet Morgan had experienced since his and Cassius's fight with the female Demigod intensified as the Dryad prince spoke of the attack on his palace a year past and his people's suspicions about what the enemy had been after. Though they had many rare items and gold in their treasury, the faint whiff of bloodcursed magic one of their mages had detected on their attackers had convinced them the staff was their primary objective.

Cassius stiffened beside Morgan as Cedric described the vision the Dryad kingdom's royal seer had seen of the battle that would unfold on Earth and the counsel she had provided her king and his court. The prince explained how he'd traveled the earthly realm for some time before landing in San Francisco a few months ago, where he'd sensed he needed to be.

"Although, truth be told, it was probably that damn thing yanking my strings all along," he muttered, eyeing the devilwood pendant darkly.

"We've discovered the name of the organization after Eden and the staff," Cassius said in the hush that followed. "Bostrof managed to plant a spy in the group. They call themselves *Ouroboros*."

Brianna frowned. "I've never heard of them."

"Never have I," Strickland said. "Are you certain of the accuracy of Bostrof's information?"

"Yes," Cassius replied.

"The only thing we don't know yet is *why* they want Eden and the staff," Morgan said.

Galliad removed a book with an ornate cover and gilded pages from inside his kaftan. "The Bloodcursed Devilwood Summoning Staff is rumored to be one of the keys used to lock Chaos in the Abyss."

"You kept that on you?" Cedric said, surprised.

"Yes. I tucked it in my loin cloth."

Cedric made a face.

Morgan clenched his jaw. Cassius's suspicion that this affair was linked to the Chester Moran incident was proving to be correct. He could practically feel the tension radiating off the Empyreal.

"A key?" Cassius said in a hard voice. "You mean, like the Eternity Key?"

Surprise widened Galliad's eyes. "You know about the Eternity Key?"

He leafed through the book, stopped on a page, and turned the volume around. Morgan stared at the imp and the glowing, golden dagger depicted on the faded pages amidst a sea of tightly packed Dryad scripture.

Brianna indicated Cassius. "The Keeper of the Eternity Key is his cat."

Galliad's jaw dropped. "What?!"

Cassius and Morgan gave the Dryad mage and the prince an abridged account of their battle with Chester Moran and his black magic sorcerers a month ago.

"So, that's what that was," Galliad murmured, pale-faced. "I felt an anomaly at the edges of the realms that night. I didn't realize it was because someone had tried to tear open the Nether." He paused, his shocked gaze on Cassius. "So, the Keeper of the Key adopted you as his master?"

"Yeah," Cassius muttered. "The others think I spoil that damn imp too much."

Morgan maintained a diplomatic silence. Cassius's kitchen cupboards were stacked full of gourmet cat food for Loki.

"Does this mean Chester and Tania's master is behind this incident too?" Strickland asked in a strained voice.

"Bostrof's spy said Rebecca likely answered to someone else," Cassius pointed out.

"Rebecca?" Brianna said, puzzled.

"That's the name used by the bloodcursed female mage who was at the bank and the magic market tonight," Morgan explained. "Bostrof's spy thinks it's not her real one."

Strickland paced the floor next to the window. "So,

are we saying these people are trying to do what Chester did? Tear open the Nether?"

A bout of sympathy danced through Morgan at his old friend's agitated tone. Chester Moran had been his protége and surrogate son. No one had been more shocked than Strickland when his true identity and intentions had finally come to light.

"I'm not sure," Cassius said uneasily.

"The Magus." Galliad was frowning at something in his book. "I was reading about this before the ghouls found us. Among the ancient fables recorded by Dryads past, one talks of a Demigod called the Magus. He was the original owner of the Bloodcursed Summoning Staff and one of the entities who helped imprison Chaos in the Abyss. It was rumored that his mother was Hecate, the Goddess of Magic."

Morgan and Cassius exchanged a startled look.

"The Demigod mage," Cassius murmured.

Galliad's frown deepened. "That woman might be related to the first Magus. It would explain why she's after the staff."

Strickland narrowed his eyes at Morgan and Cassius. "By the way, Adrianne told me something real interesting about you two tonight."

"I knew she'd tattle," Morgan grumbled.

A muscle jumped in Strickland's jawline. "When were the two of you going to inform me that you are Demigods?"

Brianna sucked in air. "What?!" She pointed at Morgan and Cassius, disbelief painted across her face. "Those two lovesick fools are Demigods?!"

"Mom," Eden murmured, embarrassed.

Cassius sighed.

Morgan scowled. "We just saved your kid's life, lady."

"'*Allies we have yet to meet,*'" Cedric quoted. He turned to Galliad, his face growing animated. "These are the people Regina must have meant when she sent me to Earth!"

"It sure looks like it," Galliad said thoughtfully.

"Not that I'm ungrateful for what you did for Eden," Brianna told Cedric frostily, "but just how long are you intending to touch my daughter's knee for?"

"*Mom!*" Eden gasped, face growing beetroot red.

CHAPTER THIRTY-THREE

"GOD, I'M TIRED," CASSIUS GROANED.

Morgan hit the light switch and closed the apartment door behind them.

It was almost dawn. They'd gone to Argonaut to help Adrianne and the others finish up the paperwork after they'd left the hospital, before finally calling it a night and telling everyone to go home.

Cassius kicked off his boots and headed into the kitchen. "Do you want a drink?"

A soft meow rose from the direction of his bedroom before Morgan could reply. Loki scampered into view, looped his body around Morgan's ankles a couple of times in greeting, and leapt into Cassius's arms.

"Hello, trouble." Cassius scratched the imp under the chin. Loki purred and headbutted his chest. "Were your ears burning tonight? 'Cause we were talking about you." He kissed the cat on the nose.

Morgan grabbed a couple of glasses from a cabinet

and poured them a shot of whiskey each, a jealous expression flitting in his eyes for a moment. Cassius swallowed a sigh. He wasn't sure whether to be flattered or worried that Morgan's possessive nature even extended to Loki.

Morgan handed the drink to Cassius. "Here."

"Thanks." He made a face. "And I kinda meant coffee."

Morgan grunted. "We're not due back at the office until the afternoon, so we should take it easy."

Loki jumped to the floor and disappeared into the bedroom. They went out onto the terrace and watched the lightening sky as they drank their whiskey.

"What do you make of what Cedric said?" Morgan finally asked Cassius.

"You mean about the Dryad seer's prediction?" Cassius swirled his glass around and stared into the amber liquid sloshing up the sides. "It worries me."

Morgan turned and leaned his back against the railing. "Because you think she's right?"

Cassius frowned. "Because I *know* she's right."

Morgan narrowed his eyes at that. "Is that your instinct talking or the other you?"

Cassius met his gaze. "Both, I think."

Morgan stared at him for a moment before blowing out a frustrated sigh. They had yet to find any information about Ivmir, the Demigod he had once been, or the identity of Cassius's past self. Cassius pursed his lips.

Maybe Bostrof is right. Maybe the answers we seek can only be found in the Spirit Realm.

"Come on, let's go to bed," Cassius murmured. "All this thinking is making my brain hurt."

Morgan followed him inside. Cassius put their empty glasses in the sink and turned to head to the bedroom. Morgan caught his hand, spun him around, and backed him up against the hallway wall.

Cassius stared, startled. "Er, Morgan?"

Morgan's hands dropped to Cassius's waist. "We still haven't discussed that little stunt you pulled at the magic market tonight." He leaned down and nipped at Cassius's chin, his tone somewhat menacing. "You know, when you broke your promise to stay close to me."

Cassius's breath hitched in his throat, desire stirring inside him at the hunger darkening Morgan's eyes. "Hmm. About that—"

Morgan swallowed the rest of his words with a scorching kiss. Cassius was rock hard in a heartbeat. He lost himself in Morgan's lips and touch, passion warming his blood. A mumbled protest left him when Morgan let go of his mouth and stripped him of his belt, his tongue half numb from Morgan's ardent sucking. He stiffened in the next instant.

Morgan had tugged his arms behind his back and was wrapping the leather strap around his wrists.

Cassius's pulse spiked on a wave of lust and anticipation. "What are you doing?"

Morgan closed his teeth on Cassius's lower lip. Cassius shuddered as he tugged on his flesh and sucked on the bite, pupils inky in a sea of blazing sapphire.

"Punishing you."

Cassius inhaled raggedly, the bulge thickening the front of his jeans growing uncomfortable. Morgan stripped him of his clothes and nudged his ankles apart with his foot.

Cassius shuddered as he stood exposed to Morgan's heated stare, legs trembling and erect cock oozing precum.

Morgan flicked the hot pearl on the quivering head with his thumb. Cassius cursed and bucked his hips, seeking the touch of the man driving him slowly out of his mind. A savage smile curved Morgan's mouth. He teased Cassius with featherlight strokes, their mouths a hairbreadth apart, their heated breaths mingling. Pleasure stiffened Cassius's body as Morgan edged him. He chewed his lip and choked back a moan.

Morgan squeezed his cock in a punishing grip.

"*Oh!*" Cassius gasped, the pleasure-pain making his hole contract.

"That's right," Morgan murmured against his throat. "Don't stifle your voice. I want to hear the sounds you make when I touch you."

Cassius dropped his head back against the wall, his cries and moans filling the hallway as he writhed and thrust his cock through Morgan's slick fingers, not caring how wanton he sounded. It wasn't long before he came, his body growing rigid and his balls rising as he exploded in Morgan's hand with a guttural shout, his soul core blazing bright.

Morgan went down on his knees, hooked Cassius's left leg over his shoulder, and slipped two cum-coated fingers inside Cassius's back passage. Cassius hissed, his hole clenching tightly around Morgan at the sudden penetration.

Morgan gritted his teeth and started thrusting in and out, stretching Cassius open with scissoring movements. Sparks exploded in front of Cassius's eyes when Morgan's fingers bumped against his swollen prostate.

"Ah! *Yes!*" Cassius panted, squeezing even tighter. "Right there!"

Morgan cursed and dropped a hand to his own straining erection. He yanked down his zipper and freed his cock. Cassius licked his lips when he saw the thick, veiny rod. He couldn't wait to have Morgan inside him. Fire filled his veins as Morgan's mouth found his half-hard shaft. Morgan teased Cassius's quivering organ with his tongue and lips for timeless moments while he rubbed his own dick and plundered Cassius's hole.

By the time he let him go and rose to his feet, Cassius was a quivering mess.

"My hands," he mumbled. "I want to touch you!"

Morgan undid the belt and dropped it to the floor along with his clothes, his chest heaving with his labored breaths. Cassius's arms found Morgan's neck as he grabbed him under his thighs and lifted him up against the wall. He wrapped his legs around Morgan's waist and angled his hips, desperate for what was to come.

"I want you in me! *Now!*" he pleaded, his heels digging insistently in Morgan's butt.

Sweat dripped down Morgan's face as he guided his

glistening cock to Cassius's opening, his eyes cobalt with passion. They both groaned when he punched inside with a hard thrust and drove in all the way to the hilt. Cassius barely had a second to adapt to the hot fullness of Morgan's penetration before Morgan drew his hips back and rocked them forward again.

"Shit!" Morgan grunted as he set the pace of their lovemaking, Cassius gasping with each powerful roll of his hips. "No matter how much we do this, each time feels like the first. Hot. Tight. And so fucking *good* I could die happy right at this moment." He pressed his mouth to the pulse thumping at the base of Cassius's throat. "I was born to be inside you!"

Incoherent sounds left Cassius as they made love with passionate savagery, the sounds their mating bodies made an erotic background to their moans and grunts, their soul cores connecting with fiery sparks. Cassius's orgasm soon raced down his spine and pooled in his belly. He came on a choked rasp that was all pleasure, his dick spurting cum between their bodies as he ejaculated.

Morgan groaned as Cassius's convulsions squeezed his swollen shaft, milking him for all he was worth. His hands found Cassius's wrists where he clung to his back. Cassius's mouth rounded on a surprised gasp as Morgan stretched his arms above his head and pinned them to the wall.

Morgan slowed and stopped, his cock throbbing inside Cassius. Cassius could tell Morgan's climax was painfully close from the way his pupils almost filled his irises. Morgan met his heated gaze and took his mouth in a blistering kiss.

"Say it," he breathed against Cassius's lips.

Cassius clenched around him. Morgan cursed and closed his eyes tight, barely hanging on to his self-control. A thrill shot through Cassius at the sight. He brought his mouth to Morgan's right ear and told him what he so desperately wanted to hear.

"Give it to me," he whispered sultrily before nipping at his lobe.

Morgan gnashed his teeth, pulled his dick halfway out of Cassius, and thrust back inside with enough force to lift him up the wall. Cassius welcomed the untamed penetration, his body accommodating the hot intruder impaling his insides, his mouth eagerly drinking Morgan's grunts as he gave in to his animal side and pounded him. Morgan stiffened when he finally crested the waves of ecstasy storming his body. He came on a feral shout, hips rising and fingers tightening punishingly on Cassius's flesh where he held his wrists, fire exploding between their soul cores.

Cassius moaned as Morgan pulsed long and deep inside him. He met Morgan's hungry gaze, his face burning at the carnal sensation of having Morgan fill him with his seed. It was a while before they stopped shuddering and twitching with aftershocks of pleasure, their hearts beating wildly against one another. Morgan let out a satisfied sigh and kissed him tenderly before carrying him into the bedroom and starting their intimate dance all over again.

CHAPTER THIRTY-FOUR

"Eden?!"

Lois stiffened in her hospital bed, eyes widening as she stared at Eden standing in the doorway of her room.

Eden swallowed and came inside before closing the door. "Hi, Lois."

Remorse swamped her as she studied her friend's pale face.

Eden and Brianna had spent most of last night talking. It was as if a dam had burst inside both of them and they'd finally been able to tell each other everything they'd kept close to their hearts for all these years. Pain, regret, anger, relief, forgiveness, love. Though she felt emotionally drained and physically exhausted after everything that had happened in the past few days, Eden was grateful to Brianna for their hours-long conversation.

For the first time in her life, she knew without a single doubt that her mother had always loved her and had done everything she could to keep her safe from the dangerous magic she had been born with. Though Brianna's efforts had been clumsy and caused her suffering, Eden realized her mother had endured an even deeper agony. She couldn't imagine a worse fate than a woman not being able to touch her own child.

Eden had cried when Brianna had told her about the attack on the Serranos. She'd wanted to see Lois straightaway. It had taken all the medical mages looking after her as well as her mother to persuade her to get some rest first.

Lois pressed her hands to her mouth, tears glimmering in her eyes. "Cassius and Morgan found you!"

She threw her covers off and struggled out of bed.

"Don't!" Eden crossed the floor, alarmed. She caught Lois just as she stumbled. "You shouldn't be moving like that!"

Lois straightened and hugged her hard.

"I was so scared," she cried against Eden's neck. "When I knew you were all alone and those—those *things* were after you, I thought I would never see you again! I'm so glad you're safe, Edie!"

Eden's vision blurred as her best friend's tears soaked into her skin. She squeezed Lois fiercely, her own tears dripping into Lois's hair. They sat on the edge of the bed and held hands, just like they'd done the last time they'd seen each other.

Lois sniffed and wiped her eyes before indicating the medallion hanging around Eden's neck. "That's new."

Eden reached for the devilwood pendant nestled against her upper chest. She could feel the silent hum of power coming from it where it warmed her skin and she sensed its deepening connection with her soul core. Since the weapon had claimed her, Cedric and Galliad had made a necklace to secure it to her body. Though the leather looked like it would snap with a simple tug, Eden knew it was practically unbreakable.

Brianna had told her what she could and couldn't reveal to Lois. Eden took a deep breath and opened her mouth.

"I know you can't tell me much about what's going on," Lois interrupted with a weak smile. "I'm just glad you're okay."

Eden deflated with a heavy sigh. *She's always been able to read my mind.*

"Is it over?" Lois said hesitantly. "Those monsters? Are they gone?"

Guilt stormed Eden at the way her friend's voice trembled.

"No. It's not over yet," she replied truthfully, squeezing Lois's fingers. "But I'm not alone this time. I have my mom and Malik and Hexa. And there's Cassius and Morgan and Argonaut. And I have... Cedric."

Her ears grew hot as the prince's name fell from her lips.

Lois stared. "Who's Cedric?"

A knock came at the door.

"Can we come in?" someone said gruffly.

Eden startled at the now achingly familiar voice.

"Yes, the door's open," Lois said, her puzzled glance shifting from Eden to the door.

Cedric walked in, an awkward expression on his face and a vase holding a gorgeous bouquet of flowers in hand. Galliad appeared behind him.

Eden swallowed a groan at the lively sparkle in the older Dryad's eyes. Galliad looked like he intended to enjoy the heck out of this situation, come what may.

"Hi there," the Dryad mage greeted jovially. "I'm Galliad, a friend of Eden's. This is Cedric." He pushed the prince forward and sent him stumbling a couple of steps. "Cedric here saved Eden's life."

A faint blush stained Lois's cheeks as she gazed wide-eyed at Cedric. "He did?"

Eden bit back a sigh. *He really is too handsome for his own good.*

Cedric flashed a scowl at Galliad before putting the vase on the bedside table.

"Hi," he said stiffly to Lois. "It's nice to meet you."

His gaze moved briefly to Eden. Eden did her best not to flush. The way Lois stared at her told her she'd failed miserably.

Lois looked between Eden and Cedric, her expression turning shrewd. "It's nice to meet you too, *Cedric.*"

Eden cursed inwardly. She'd forgotten how much of a romantic her best friend was.

"Those flowers," she said, going for the distraction tactic. "I haven't seen them before."

She touched the white and purple blooms in the

vase. Green light flashed on her fingers and lit up the petals.

Lois gasped. "Oh!"

"That's because they're from the Dryad kingdom," Cedric muttered.

Eden's eyes widened. "You made these?!"

The tips of Cedric's ears grew red.

"Indeed he did," Galliad gushed. "Isn't His Highness simply amazing?"

Cedric cut his eyes to the mage.

"Stop being so fake," he said between gritted teeth. "A five-year old Dryad can do that."

"*His Highness?!*" Lois hissed at Eden.

Eden wished a hole would open up in the floor and swallow her whole. Judging from Cedric's face, he was thinking the same thing.

"Cedric is the second prince of the Dryad kingdom," Galliad explained gallantly. "He has been a knight in shining armor to our young Eden since the fateful night they met."

"You spent the night with him?!" Lois squeaked, eyes bulging.

Eden groaned and dropped her face in her hands. "It wasn't like that."

"What *was* it like, Your Highness?" Galliad simpered.

"I am so close to kicking your ass right now!" Cedric growled at the mage.

Lois blinked at the glowering prince. She leaned sideways.

"So, you like the gorgeous but grumpy type, huh?" she asked Eden in a conspiratorial whisper.

Eden groaned some more. Another knock came at the door. It opened to reveal Adrianne and Julia. Eden tensed.

"We're leaving soon," the sorceress said with a friendly smile.

Lois turned to Eden, her face serious. "Is everything okay?"

Eden hugged her close. "I need to go with them. I'll see you soon. Say hi to your mom and dad and Josh for me."

Lois stiffened slightly before squeezing her back. "Stay safe."

Her gaze followed Eden as she headed out of the room with Cedric and Galliad.

CHAPTER THIRTY-FIVE

Cassius gripped his cell tightly. "Any news from Karl?"

Morgan glanced at Cassius as they rolled into the underground garage under the Argonaut bureau. He was on the phone with Bostrof.

Cassius frowned. "Alright. Let me know if anything else crops up." He ended the call and gazed blindly through the windshield as Morgan parked the SUV. "Karl thinks *Ouroboros* is about to make some kind of move. We're still nowhere near finding out what they want with Eden and the devilwood staff though."

"We'll get there." Morgan stepped out of the vehicle. "Be patient."

They bumped into Charlie in the elevator.

"How's everything coming along?" Morgan said. "Will we be ready in time?"

"Yes," Charlie replied distractedly.

"What's wrong?" Cassius murmured.

Charlie hesitated. "Are you sure this is gonna work?"

Morgan patted him lightly on the back. "We have every confidence in your abilities, kid."

"You can do it," Cassius said with a reassuring smile.

The elevator door pinged open on the tenth floor.

"Oh." Charlie blinked. "This isn't where I wanted to be."

"Did you get *any* sleep last night?" Cassius said as he and Morgan stepped out into the agency's main office area.

"No." The enchanter pressed a button on the panel. "Judging from the hickey on your neck, neither did you. I'll see you guys later."

The elevator door closed on him.

Cassius tucked his collar up and frowned at Morgan. "I thought I told you not to mark me in obvious places."

Morgan shrugged, unabashed. "That's your punishment for leaving me hanging yesterday." He paused. "Is it me or is Charlie getting more bold?"

Cassius rolled his eyes. "The kid was always bold. You guys just didn't realize it until now."

They headed to the conference room where they'd arranged to meet Strickland and the others. To their surprise, Brianna and Malik were there too.

"They make it to the safe house okay?" Cassius asked Adrianne.

The sorceress nodded. "Yeah. Zach and Bailey are with them right now. Galliad went to Chinatown to sort out his shop and send a message to the Dryad king. He'll join them later."

"He's intending to stay with Cedric and Eden?" Brianna asked, surprised.

"Yes," Strickland replied. "He insisted. I agreed. Galliad is the Dryad kingdom's most powerful mage. It makes sense to have him protecting those two."

Malik frowned. "Still, this affair concerns Hexa and Argonaut. We are more than capable of safeguarding Eden without having to involve the Dryad kingdom."

"They are already knee-deep in this mess, what with their prince being in our city," Strickland said. "And the Bloodcursed Devilwood Summoning Staff technically belongs to them."

"*Ouroboros*'s magic is not to be trifled with," Julia told Malik. "It's been some time since I've come across a mage as powerful as that woman. We could do with all the help we can get."

"Lest we forget, that woman's also a Demigod." Adrianne looked curiously at Cassius and Morgan. "By the way, I didn't know Demis could wield magic. Or take on the appearance of angels."

"From what we know of their history, they shouldn't be able to use magic." Cassius frowned. "But, then again, Chester shouldn't have been able to tear a hole in the Nether either. As for having wings, I think angels and Demis share many similarities."

A somber hush followed.

"You okay?" Morgan asked Brianna. "Your eyes look puffy."

"I'm fine," Brianna said dismissively. She studied

them with an uneasy expression. "How certain are you that there's a mole in Hexa?"

"I'm positive, now more than ever," Cassius stated adamantly. "After last night's attack, it's clear that, whoever the spy is, they have intimate knowledge of your history."

"The bloodcursed mage told Eden you would have killed her when she was born if you'd known the dire fate that awaited her," Morgan explained in a hard voice.

Brianna paled. "She said that?!"

Cassius nodded. "Which means *Ouroboros* knows everything. That Eden was born with bloodcursed magic. That you and Hexa bound her powers when she was a baby. I suspect they even knew she wouldn't be able to wield her magic until the devilwood staff absorbed her blood and accepted her as its mage. They've been waiting, all this time."

"The only thing they couldn't anticipate was where the staff would appear in this realm," Morgan said. "They tried to get to it before it arrived on Earth. Unfortunately, their actions in the Dryad kingdom only precipitated the inevitable."

"And they couldn't have known Cedric would be its guardian or that your daughter would plan to run away from home," Cassius added. "They missed her at Lois's house and have been on her tail since."

Strickland drummed his fingers on the table. "They must have been watching Eden her entire life."

"Waiting for the opportune time to strike," Julia muttered darkly.

Adrianne grimaced. "That's creepy."

Brianna's knuckles whitened on the table. "So, I can't protect her? After everything Eden and I have sacrificed to keep her safe all these years, you're telling me I can't protect my own daughter from these people?!"

Her voice echoed around the conference room, full of anger and frustration.

Malik laid a hand on her shoulder. "That's not what they're saying, Brianna. We need to understand how these people work if we want to defeat them. Now that we know they've infiltrated our organization and have been monitoring Eden's every movement, it gives us a chance to strike back."

"He's right," Strickland said gruffly.

Brianna was silent for some time.

"There are a dozen people in the whole of Hexa who know about Eden's magic and her spellbound soul core," she said finally. "Five of them are in the San Francisco bureau. I don't want to believe any of them would want to hurt my daughter."

"We'll soon find out if you're right," Cassius murmured.

Brianna stared, confusion dawning on her face.

"What do you mean?" Malik said.

CHAPTER THIRTY-SIX

The woman's nails dug into her palms as her master's voice rang in her ears, fury a bubbling pit in her stomach. "I'm sorry. I promise, I won't let you down again."

The man's face fluttered in the looking glass. His reflection danced across the cracked surfaces of the mirrors surrounding her, his features hazy. The only things she could make out were his eyes. They were dark and piercing and filled with the knowledge of a life long-lived.

She did not know his real identity. The only thing she was certain of was that he was her savior. It was thanks to him that she'd discovered who she was and the magic she had been born to wield. The fact that the Bloodcursed Devilwood Summoning Staff was destined for another was an obstacle they would soon overcome. Determination filled her once more.

Once I absorb Eden's soul core, I'll be able to control the staff.

"I hope you keep your word this time," the man said mildly. "I will not tolerate more failures."

She sensed the threat behind his words and suppressed a shiver. "Rest assured, master. I shall locate their hideout and have Eden and the bloodcursed staff in my grasp before dawn."

"I will hold you to that promise. Contact me when you have them."

The communication spell dissipated. The man's face faded, as did the daunting aura of his presence. She waited until he was truly gone before storming out of the abandoned building she and *Ouroboros* had taken up temporary residence in.

The ghouls who served her and her most trusted sorcerers looked up as she descended the steps to the overgrown yard, their eyes crimson with the powerful bloodcursed magic she had gifted them with.

"Let's go."

CEDRIC FOUND EDEN PERCHED ON A WINDOWSILL IN THE drawing room, her chin resting atop her knees.

He closed the door with one foot and carried the steaming mugs he held across the room. "You should stay away from there."

She unfolded her legs and straightened as she watched him cross the floor.

Cedric's chest tightened at her downcast

expression. It still seemed incredible that he had come to care for her so much in the little time they'd known one another. Though he'd done his best to deny his initial attraction to Eden, nearly losing her last night had made it all too clear exactly how he felt about her. He saw no point in fighting what his soul core was telling him.

He wondered if Regina the Seer had foreseen this too. Maybe that was the reason she had chosen him out of the four princes of the Dryad kingdom for this particular mission.

He handed Eden the herbal tea he'd prepared and leaned against the window frame opposite her. "Don't look so disheartened."

Eden's hand rose to the devilwood pendant resting against her chest. She fiddled with it anxiously. "Is this really going to work? Us hiding here while Argonaut and Hexa try and find that woman and *Ouroboros*?"

Cedric shrugged. "Honestly? I don't know. But it's the only plan we have right now. At least we aren't on our own anymore."

They studied the landscape outside the window.

The safe house Argonaut had brought them to was located in the hills, in the middle of the city. A tower dominated the skyline to the east, metal gleaming in the fading sunlight. The woodland surrounding the property was already growing dark, the bright rays barely penetrating the thick foliage.

Footsteps rose in the hallway.

Bailey opened the drawing room door. "How are you two holding up?"

"We're fine, thanks," Eden murmured.

Bailey made a face. "No need to lie, kid. I hope you like tacos 'cause that's what we're having for dinner. Your mom is coming over with some stuff for you." He looked over at Cedric. "Galliad called. He said he's been delayed by something. He'll be here later tonight."

"Where's Zach?" Cedric said, curious.

"Around." Bailey waved a hand vaguely. The doorbell rang. Faint lines marred the wizard's brow. "That was quick."

Cedric and Eden accompanied him out into the hall.

"This place sure seems to be on everyone's radar for a safe house," Cedric muttered.

"Relax, we've got this. Besides, this location is only revealed to people Argonaut trusts implicitly." Bailey checked the peephole. He frowned. "That's odd."

He opened the door warily, his hand rising to the rune-covered dagger on his belt. Malik stood on the threshold, a suitcase in hand and a grumpy expression on his face. Valerie was at his side.

"Hi, Eden," the aide said with a warm smile.

"Hi, Valerie." Eden peered past their shoulders. "Where's mom?"

"She went by the office first," Malik said. "She shouldn't be long."

Bailey gazed suspiciously out at the front yard and driveway. He studied Malik and Valerie with a guarded expression as they came inside the house. "We made it clear that only people Argonaut approved of could know the address of this place."

"Brianna got Strickland's permission," Malik retorted. "You can ring your bureau and check if you want." His expression softened as he looked at Eden. "Where's your bedroom?"

Cedric held out a hand for the suitcase. "I can take that up."

Eden sighed. "I'm not an invalid."

She took the case and headed upstairs, her back stiff.

Cedric turned to find Malik frowning at him. "What?"

"You better stay away from her," the sorcerer warned.

Cedric narrowed his eyes. "Last time I checked, you weren't her father. And Eden is more than old enough to make her own decisions."

"That might be the case in your kingdom, but this is Earth and Eden is still a minor," Malik grated out.

"Now, now, children," Bailey said in a conciliatory tone, "how about I make everyone a drink?"

"I'm driving," Malik snapped.

"Eden is underage," Cedric growled.

Bailey sighed. "Alright, how about a coffee then? I have just the—"

A crash came from upstairs. Eden screamed.

Fear drenched Cedric in a cold sweat.

He had a foot on the bottom step of the staircase when a grunt had him spinning around. Malik gazed at him dazedly before looking down at the dagger embedded in his heart. A red spray filled the air as Valerie slashed Bailey's throat with a blade throbbing with bloodcursed magic. The wizard made a choked sound and clutched the gaping wound, blood pouring between his fingers and splashing heavily onto the floor.

Both men collapsed in a crimson pool.

A sound at the top of the stairs drew Cedric's stunned gaze. His eyes widened. The bloodcursed mage stood holding Eden's arm in a cruel grip, ghouls and sorcerers crowding around them.

She looked past Cedric, her expression triumphant. "You have done well, sister."

A faint smile tilted Valerie's lips. "Lucille."

"Valerie?!" Eden mumbled, pale-faced.

"I'm sorry, Eden," the aide said, her expression cool.

Cedric's heart raced with a mixture of rage and despair. "Let her go!"

He snatched the wand at his back and started up the stairs, the weapon transforming into the laurel staff.

Scarlet bands throbbing with bloodcursed magic wrapped around his legs and arms and sent him stumbling against the banister. He fell to his knees, his shins scraping against the steps.

Valerie dragged him down the stairs.

Cedric kicked out, frustration gnawing at him. Magic flared on his staff where it lay trapped at his side. Two green spheres flashed into existence. He cast the spell bombs at the witch with his will.

A shimmering red shield fell in front of Valerie.

The spell bombs bounced off it and smashed through the wall on the left. An explosion ripped through the property as something detonated inside the kitchen. Debris and smoke filled the air. The lights in the hall flickered and went out.

Valerie glared at Cedric. "Thanks, sister."

The restraints holding him captive tightened until they bit punishingly into his skin, drawing blood. He gritted his teeth against the burning pain of bloodcursed magic.

"Bring him along," Lucille ordered with a sneer. "Our Eden here seems to care for him. I'm sure he'll prove useful as a hostage."

CHAPTER THIRTY-SEVEN

"How far out are we?" Cassius asked tensely.

"Four miles," Julia replied crisply.

"Any response from Zach or Bailey?" Morgan said.

"Not yet."

They headed past Buena Vista park and Corona Heights, a procession of Argonaut and Hexa tactical vehicles on their tail. Sutro Hill appeared in the distance. A thin trail of smoke danced toward the darkening sky above the treetops crowding the elevation and the immense metal tower dominating it.

Cassius clenched his fists. *Please be okay!*

This had been his plan. He just hoped Eden and Cedric let him off the hook afterward for using them as pawns in his trap.

"Looks like *Ouroboros* took the bait," Brianna declared grimly.

"His Majesty is going to have my guts for garters when he finds out I put the prince's life in danger," Galliad grumbled.

"Cedric isn't a kid," Morgan said gruffly. "Besides, he would have wanted to be with Eden."

"We couldn't tell them this was our idea," Cassius explained. "Their reactions needed to be genuine to convince *Ouroboros*."

"I sure hope this scheme of yours works," the Dryad muttered.

"As do I," Brianna said darkly. "I'll never forgive myself if something happens to my daughter."

Cassius squashed his own misgivings and studied the witch where they sat in the Argonaut van. "You know the only way to keep her safe is to see this through. The bloodcursed mage will never leave Eden alone if we don't get rid of her once and for all."

An overwrought look clouded Brianna's face. "I understand that. But she's my child, Cassius. I just wish I could have taken her place!"

"Hang on." Adrianne pressed her earpiece and accepted an incoming call where she sat manning the command station in the back of the van with Julia. "Bostrof? You have a location?" She listened before tapping out coordinates into the computer. "Thanks." She ended the call. A map of San Francisco opened up on the monitor. "Karl got in touch with Bostrof. Maggie also sent a message. The command signal that took out the cameras in the bank last night came from the same address Karl just gave to Bostrof."

She pointed at the screen. They stared at a flashing red dot on the coastline, southwest of their position.

"Send the details to the teams following us,"

Morgan ordered. "Tell them to go ahead and secure the perimeter."

The gates leading to the safe house were wide open when they turned the corner of the rise. They stormed up the driveway toward the burning building at the end and the two figures slouched outside it. Cassius jumped out of the vehicle with the others, his pulse racing with dread. Relief flooded him as the men rose to their feet.

Adrianne closed the distance to Bailey, her expression anxious. "Are you alright?"

"I'm fine." The wizard grimaced and touched his neck. "That was one hell of an illusion. It really felt like that woman slashed my throat."

Brianna stopped in front of Malik, her expression troubled. "You're not hurt?"

The sorcerer shook his head. "No. The enchantment worked. Valerie thinks I'm dead."

He startled when she pressed a hand to his chest.

Relief brightened Brianna's eyes. "That's good." Her face hardened. "So, she was *Ouroboros*'s informant after all."

"She's not just an informant." Malik looked over at Cassius and Morgan, a muscle jumping in his jawline. "The bloodcursed mage's name is Lucille. She's Valerie's sister."

"What?!" Brianna gasped.

Cassius frowned. Valerie was supposed to be a Level Three witch. He hadn't detected any trace of her sister's bloodcursed magic when she'd been in their presence last night.

She must be masking her abilities. She's probably closer to being a Level One magic user.

"Did Charlie and Zach follow them?" Morgan asked Bailey.

"Yeah. *Ouroboros* used a portal to space-jump out of here." The wizard made a face. "I'm surprised Charlie agreed to fly with Zach."

"He didn't really have a choice in the matter. He needs to stay close to them for our plan to work." Morgan studied the flames gushing out of the house. "This part of Charlie's enchantment too?"

"Er, no." Bailey made a face. "One of Cedric's spell bombs took out a gas line."

"Shit."

"Ten bucks says Strickland takes this out of our paychecks," Adrianne muttered morosely.

❦

EDEN'S HEART THUMPED VIOLENTLY AGAINST HER RIBS AS Lucille dragged her out of the gateway, her head spinning from the breakneck journey. Sand and dirt shifted under her feet as they emerged under a dazzling, star-lit sky. Wind soughed through the towering, dark structures rising around her. The sound of crashing surf rose up ahead, where the land dropped precipitously.

They were in the grounds of an abandoned amusement park, on a cliff overlooking the ocean. Distant lights shimmered to the north, too far to call for help.

Valerie appeared from the portal ahead of the ghouls and sorcerers. She cast her charge unceremoniously to the ground. A grunt left Cedric as he landed in the dirt, his arms and legs bound by magic still.

"Let him go!" Eden snarled.

She made to move toward the Dryad.

Lucille tugged viciously on her arm, causing her to stumble. "I don't think so. Now, why don't you be a good girl and come with me?"

Eden's eyes widened when she saw where Lucille was leading her. It was a large, circular pit in the middle of the amusement park. Judging from the rows of seats making up the tiered levels of the arena, it used to be a show stage of sorts. A stone platform stood in the center. The *Ouroboros* sorcerers were putting the finishing touches on a magic circle taking up most of the surface.

"What the hell is that?!" Cedric growled.

Valerie had used her magic to lift him upright and bring him along, his feet raking the dirt where he was dragged forcibly beside her.

"Why, I thought that would be clear," the witch said mockingly. "It's a sacrificial ritual. Your girlfriend is about to get her soul core ripped out of her body."

Lucille registered Eden and Cedric's horrified expressions with a chuckle. "Don't take it personally. She was just unlucky to be born with bloodcursed magic. I need her soul core to wield the Bloodcursed Devilwood Summoning Staff. The weapon was wrongly destined to be hers when it should have been mine all along. As for you, my Dryad prince, your organs will fetch a fortune on the black market. Why, the heart of a royal is an ingredient most alchemists would sell their first-born child for."

Rage filled Eden as Lucille and Valerie's demented laughter rose to the sky.

The devilwood pendant trembled against her skin, the weapon glowing crimson with her wrath.

CHAPTER THIRTY-EIGHT

Cassius and Morgan flew fast and low over the land, Julia keeping pace with them. A Ferris wheel rose out of the gloom ahead, its outline stark against the backdrop of the ocean glimmering under the stars.

They found Charlie and Zach atop it.

The enchanter looked pale where he clung to one of the metal beams connecting the passenger car to the wheel, knuckles white and wind ruffling his dark hair.

Cassius alighted soundlessly beside them and folded his wings. "You guys okay?"

The car trembled slightly as Morgan and Julia landed next to him.

"We're peachy," Zach muttered, his attention directed at something in the landscape below them.

Cassius followed the demon's gaze. He clenched his jaw.

Eden stood tied to a pole in the middle of a stage, in a sunken arena within the grounds of the abandoned amusement park. The bloodcursed mage was talking to

Valerie outside the magic circle etched onto the stone platform. Cedric stood guarded by ghouls and sorcerers a short distance from them, his arms and legs bound by magic.

Cassius took a shallow breath and sent out a faint pulse of seraphic energy.

It took but seconds for him to map out the location of the enemy around them. The Argonaut and Hexa agents were where Morgan and Adrianne had instructed them to stand by, around the boundaries of the park. Though they more than matched their foe numbers-wise, the bloodcursed magic Lucille could bestow upon her sorcerers and ghouls to augment their abilities meant they would be twice as strong as the average Argonaut or Hexa agent. And Lucille and Valerie would be the hardest to take down.

Cassius detected several powerful soul cores approaching from the east. It was Adrianne and the others. They were only a couple of minutes away.

Crimson light flared below.

Cedric cursed, his voice reaching them faintly as he struggled against his bonds, heedless of the monsters growling at him and the sorcerers threatening him with spell bombs. His gaze was locked on Eden where she was bathed in the red luminescence of the runes coming to life around her. Lucille crossed the stage toward the young girl, her hands and eyes aglow with bloodcursed magic.

"It's time," Cassius said grimly.

Morgan gave the command through their comm link just as Charlie removed the Altered Mind box he'd been clutching under his arm. He cast it into the air and activated the enchantment.

♨

DESPAIR FILLED EDEN AS SHE STRUGGLED AGAINST THE iron chains fixing her hands and feet to the wooden stake. The shackles had been imbued with black magic and lay heavily upon her flesh, the metal burning into her skin. Though they hurt like they had in the attack back at the underground market, the power inside her soul core and the devilwood pendant were keeping the pain at bay.

The stone platform grew hot beneath her as bloodcursed magic flooded the stage, the spell making the air shimmer with a red haze. Lucille advanced toward her, her expression jubilant. Crimson spheres formed above her palms, the light reflecting the evil radiating from her eyes.

Eden didn't need to be a magic user to sense the immense energy pulsing from Valerie's sister. It throbbed against her skin and put her teeth on edge. The devilwood pendant whined faintly as it danced against her chest, its bloodlust all too clear. It wanted to fight the enemy before them. She clenched her jaw.

Dammit! It will only activate if it drinks my blood. I need to find a way to cut my skin!

Lucille stopped in front of her. "I hear this only hurts for a moment. So my master tells me anyway."

Eden tensed, not liking where this was going.

The bloodcursed mage arched an eyebrow, scarlet

pupils studying Eden as if she were an insect. "I can't really see the point of prolonging your suffering, so I will make this quick, little girl."

Her eyes flared.

Eden gasped as the bloodcursed mage punched her hands inside her body, her fingers sinking beneath Eden's skin as if she were made of mist. Fire exploded in her belly, so sudden and so sharp it brought tears to her eyes.

Eden bit her lip and swallowed a cry, determined not to show her agony to the woman torturing her. A strange sound reached her ears above the dull ringing in her skull. It took a couple of seconds for her to make out what it was.

Someone was playing music.

The flames scorching Eden's insides abated as Lucille withdrew her hands and stepped back, a frown darkening her face.

Lights exploded around them. The muted roar of a crowd followed.

Lucille cursed. Eden stared.

The amusement park was coming to life, the broken rides fixed and restored to their former glory even as they watched. People appeared in the grounds, their insubstantial shapes solidifying out of thin air. They crowded the attractions and filled the alleys between colorful booths and stalls, heedless of the growling ghouls and the confused sorcerers among them. The laughter of children rose in the night.

"What's going on?" Valerie called out from beyond the stage, her voice laced with panic.

"I don't know," Lucille replied in a hard voice. "Calm down, sister. This is an enchantment. It can't hurt—"

A gurgled shout cut the air. One of the sorcerers went flying into a food stand, blood blossoming from the cuts on his chest and face. Zach appeared from amidst the crowd of oblivious revelers, a Stark Steel sword and a lasso of water in hand.

"*You!*" Lucille spat.

A ghoul screeched next to the Haunted House. Another sorcerer yelled out somewhere close to the Ferris wheel.

"What's going on?!" Lucille barked.

Adrianne came into view, bright spell bombs hovering above her palms.

"Why, I believe we are kicking your ass," the sorceress said with a scowl.

Valerie gaped at the wizard who stepped out from behind her. "You—?! But—*but I killed you!*"

The defensive shield Bailey had erected around himself and Adrianne blocked an attack from a sorcerer. "It'll take more than that to get rid of me, witch!"

Julia shot up from the ground next to the Drop Tower, two sorcerers dangling in her grip. She dropped them on the ride before diving for the ghouls fighting Galliad.

Lucille's contemptuous gaze skimmed over Morgan's team and the Dryad mage. "You can't beat me! I am a Demigod!"

"We can't." A savage smile curved Zach's mouth. He

looked up, his pupils crimson with demonic power. "But *they* sure can."

A bright storm detonated above the stage. It smashed into Lucille and cast her some thirty feet into the air. A harsh cry left her as she crashed into the stands west of the arena, plastic benches and concrete giving way beneath her.

The radiance surrounding Cassius and the tempest engulfing Morgan washed over Eden in strong waves as they straightened from where they'd dropped onto the platform, their Demigod forms on full display. Morgan headed over to her and sliced the chains binding her to the stake, his sword of black wind shivering with power.

"Are you hurt?" the dark-winged angel growled.

Eden swallowed and shook her head, her pulse hammering in her veins. She rubbed the fresh marks on her wrists and looked dazedly at the Argonaut and Hexa agents using the cover of the enchanted crowd to storm the grounds of the amusement park.

"How did you find us?!"

"*We laid a trap at the safe house.*" Cassius's gaze locked on Lucille. "*I'll explain later.*"

The bloodcursed mage was rising above the stands, a shimmering crimson sphere surrounding her floating body, her dark hair fluttering wildly around her head.

Eden's ears popped as the pressure around them plummeted.

Sinister magic exploded across the amusement park, drenching the air in a red mist wreathed with shadows. The Argonaut and Hexa agents engaging the sorcerers and ghouls startled as their enemy became shrouded in a scarlet light.

"Raise your shields!" Morgan roared. "Do not fight them one on one!"

Lucille charged toward Cassius. The Empyreal shot up to meet her, lightning erupting around him and stone cracking beneath his feet.

They clashed in mid-air. The impact boomed across the park and rattled the metal rides. Morgan snapped his wings open and rose to join the two blurred figures engaged in a deadly fight high above the ground, his body wrapped in inky currents.

Valerie climbed onto the stage, her gaze full of loathing. "Give me the pendant!"

Eden stiffened, hand rising to clasp the medallion. A pale flash caught her eye.

An enormous shape was bounding down the stands toward them. It sprung onto the stone platform. A giant white tigress with blazing blue eyes skidded to a stop between them.

"Mom?!" she mumbled.

She'd heard of her mother's transformation magic. She had never witnessed it before. But there was no denying the familiar magic emanating from the powerful beast gazing at her.

"Show me what you can do, daughter," Brianna growled, her hackles rising as she turned to face Valerie.

Eden swallowed. Determination filled her. She grabbed the devilwood pendant where it lay against her breastbone and sliced a cut across her palm. The weapon flared crimson as it absorbed her blood. It detached from the necklace that bound it and transformed into the dark staff. Bloodcursed magic swelled inside her, flooding her blood and bones to the brim. The devilwood staff hummed in her grip, its power melding seamlessly with hers, the sound it made almost gleeful.

Crimson lines exploded across Eden's skin. Red static sparked around her.

She levitated above the stage, her gaze finding the sorcerers surrounding Cedric.

CHAPTER THIRTY-NINE

Cedric rolled and narrowly avoided the spell bomb that smashed into the spot where he'd just been. Dust and fragments of concrete rained down on him. Something sharp sliced a cut across his right cheek. He scowled, swiped the legs out from under the sorcerer who'd attacked him, and grappled for the knife at the man's waist with his boots, his gaze shifting briefly to the laurel staff lying some fifteen feet from his head.

"Come to me!" he yelled.

The weapon trembled and moved across the ground under his will, the runes on the wood shimmering green. Relief flooded him when it came within his grasp.

Heat flared on his arm as a ghoul took a swipe at him.

A spell bomb brimming with Dryad magic took a chunk out of the monster's face before it could sink its teeth into Cedric.

Galliad appeared, the mage leaping across the stands to reach him. "Your Highness!"

Cedric maneuvered himself onto his front and climbed to his feet. Movement flickered to his right. A gasp left him as he leaned sharply out of the way of the claws swinging for his eyes. He stumbled and would have fallen were it not for the hand that clutched his back and steadied him.

The air trembled with power as Eden alighted beside him.

She sent the ghouls and sorcerers closing in on them flying through the air with a swing of her arm, her blonde hair dancing around her head and her eyes a bright crimson. The magic shackles binding Cedric fell away with a single touch of her hand.

Eden caressed his face, a concerned frown wrinkling her brow as she traced the light wound on his cheek. "Are you hurt?"

Cedric shivered at the raw magic oozing from her very pores. "No."

He clasped her fingers and brought them to his lips, his soul core shuddering as it welcomed the bloodcursed power of the one it had deemed his mate. Eden's mouth parted on a sharp inhale, pupils dilating with awareness.

Someone cleared their throat.

Cedric turned to find Galliad gazing at them with a mildly amused expression.

"Not that this isn't a welcome development, but we have more urgent matters to attend to, Your Highness."

Malik scowled behind the mage.

MORGAN DEFLECTED A VOLLEY OF BLOODCURSED SPELL bombs with his swords. The red spheres vanished toward the sky before exploding harmlessly a few hundred feet above him. He cursed when another three detonated next to him. Wind roared as he was shoved violently sideways, the dark currents protecting him from the blasts.

Sparks exploded up ahead. Cassius had slammed his sword into the shield protecting the bloodcursed mage where they hovered above the amusement park. Though the barrier trembled, it did not shatter, the woman's magic resisting the angel's lightning-wreathed, Stark Steel blade. She bared her teeth, her pupils flaring red.

Morgan scowled and winged his way over, his heart racing. It seemed killing a Demigod would be no easy task.

We have to find a way to break through that wall! We might gain the upper hand if I pierce her soul core with my sword!

Alarm jolted him. Lassoes of crimson magic had darted out of the bloodcursed mage's sphere. They encircled Cassius even as he moved out of the way, trapping his wings and arms against his body. A tendril snaked up the angel's chest and wrapped around his throat. Cassius frowned, his eyes brightening with a burst of seraphic energy that made the air tremble.

The pressure wave slowed Morgan down a fraction. Fear squeezed his heart as the tether tightened around

Cassius's neck. The Empyreal gritted his teeth and fought the bloodcursed magic trying to strangle the breath out of him.

Fury burned Morgan. He was at Cassius's side in a flash.

The black sword whined again and again as he dropped it upon the magic restraints, inky wind shredding the crimson cords. The dark currents dissipated seconds later. Morgan clenched his jaw.

The ropes were repairing themselves.

Lucille laughed, a sound full of madness.

"*Ivmir!*" Cassius grated out with a wince of pain. "*Take my hand!*"

Morgan did as Cassius commanded, aware that the Demigod dwelling inside the Empyreal was the one who had spoken. Their fingers met with a flash of heat that echoed straight through to his soul core.

"*Do you trust me?*"

Morgan blinked, startled by what he read in Cassius's eyes. "Always."

Cassius's pupils flared with dazzling light. "*Then do not fight this, my love.*"

Confusion slammed into Morgan. Time slowed, the brightness emanating from Cassius filling his world. A name fluttered through his consciousness, one he grasped for a single heartbeat before pain gripped his skull and cast it to the winds once more.

Air locked in his throat with his next breath, the fire piercing his soul so sudden and so violent he could only gasp.

"*Awaken!*"

The command echoed in Morgan's skull, the voice of his Demigod lover full of an authority that would not be denied. The blaze bloomed inside him, flooding his body with a force that was both alien and yet hauntingly familiar. His eyes rounded.

This—this isn't seraphic energy!

"Embrace it, Ivmir!" Cassius choked out. *"This is also your power to wield!"*

The magic that flooded Morgan's veins and tempered his flesh and bones smelled fresh and green, like an ancient, untouched forest. Emerald sparks exploded on his fingertips. They danced across his skin and down his dark sword, bringing forth green shoots. The weapon thickened and lengthened, viridescent light fluttering among the inky currents and the leaves forming between them.

A crown of black wind and oak grew on Morgan's head.

He inhaled deeply, savoring the raw magic swelling inside him. It was warm and welcoming, like a friend he had not met in a long time.

"What is this?!" Lucille snarled.

Morgan ignored her and wielded the sword of wind once more. The blade carved through the bloodcursed shackles strangling Cassius, destroying them before they had a chance to regenerate.

Lucille cursed. *"Impossible!* No power in this world can counter mine!"

A scream sounded far below them.

The bloodcursed mage froze within her crimson sphere, shock widening her eyes.

Brianna had brought Valerie down, her white fur matted with blood and her enormous chest heaving from her battle with the witch, a giant paw pressed against the fallen woman's squirming body. Gurgling sounds left Valerie as she tried to stem the flow of blood from the wound on her throat, the color draining rapidly from her face.

"*Valerie!*" Lucille screamed.

Shadows exploded around the mage as she dove.

"Shit!" Morgan followed her, Cassius hot on his tail.

They both recognized the stench of black magic mixing with her bloodcursed powers.

Brianna shifted to her human form and glared at the approaching mage. Magic exploded on her hands as she braced for battle.

A figure blurred in front of her.

Eden raised the devilwood staff, fury darkening her features. The spell bomb she cast slammed Lucille out of the sky and sent her crashing into the House of Mirrors.

CHAPTER FORTY

"Eden!" Brianna gasped.

"I'm okay, mom. I need to finish this."

She ignored Brianna's protest and shot toward the gaping hole in the building where Lucille had disappeared, power thrumming through her. The enchantment magic engulfing the amusement park was fading, the noisy crowd and lights fading to reveal the run-down remains.

The House of Mirrors soared before her, its crumbling walls pale under the starlight. Eden entered the shadowy interior.

A volley of crimson spheres came at her from the right and left.

Eden blocked them with a grunt, the barrier she'd erected wavering under the magic trying to tear through it.

Someone caught her before she hit the wall.

"*Careful,*" Cassius warned in a low voice, his white wings bright in the gloom. "*This isn't just Lucille's powers anymore."*

Morgan appeared beside them. Surprise darted through Eden at the sight of the crown on his head and the sword of wind's new look.

She recognized the magic rippling across the blade. "What happened to you?"

"We'll explain later," Morgan said dismissively.

A faint noise came from the murky space before them. They tensed as a red mist wreathed with black magic washed over them.

"That scent," Eden said warily. "Is that her master?"

"*Yes.*" Cassius frowned. "*This is what we sensed when Chester Moran was possessed by him.*"

Eden clenched her jaw. She drew forth a ball of white light and cast it into the darkness. Glass glinted in the twilight. Dozens of Lucilles appeared as the orb brightened, the mage's reflections fractured by the broken mirrors lining the chamber.

A wall of bloodcursed spell bombs burst into life and accelerated toward Eden and the two angels. They scattered, the magic missing them by inches.

"*You will pay!*" Lucille hissed. "I will make you suffer for Valerie's death! You will rue the day you were born, you insolent—!"

The mirrors exploded in a green-tinted, inky storm.

The bloodcursed mage gasped as Cassius's lightning-wrapped blade found her back, her position revealed. Crimson magic tainted with shadows flared around her, protecting her from the black blade that sought to pierce her next.

Cassius and Morgan harmonized their attack, their

weapons blurring as they slashed at Lucille. None of their strikes reached her. Manic laughter bubbled from the bloodcursed mage's throat.

Eden shivered. The voice coming from Lucille was no longer her own. She sensed the sinister aura of another inside the woman.

"How foolish!" The bloodcursed mage's crimson gaze danced over the two angels glowering at her before finding Eden. "Now, grant me my prize, child. Your soul core and that staff belong to me."

Lucille headed for her, the air shivering and the building trembling under the dark power flowing from her. Cassius cursed as he tried to follow, his movements sluggish in the hold of the shadows restraining him. Morgan tore at them with his black blade, his face furious.

We must kill her, mistress.

Eden startled. She looked around wildly for the source of the voice that had just spoken to her.

There was no one there.

She realized it had come from inside her skull.

"Who—who are you?!"

I am the weapon you wield.

She stared at the devilwood staff in her hand.

"How?" Eden mumbled. "How do we kill her?!"

I am not called a summoning staff for nothing.

❦

CASSIUS'S HEART POUNDED AS MORGAN FINALLY FREED him from the black magic holding him captive. They shot toward Lucille. His neck prickled when they got within twenty feet of the mage. Goosebumps broke out on his flesh.

He grabbed Morgan's arm and stayed his charge.

Morgan jerked to a halt with a harsh grunt. "What are you—?!"

Blinding light detonated up ahead.

They squinted at the crimson-tinged brightness, wings flaring to slow their bodies as they were shoved back some dozen feet. Cassius's pulse raced wildly as he peered into the dazzling brilliance.

"What the hell is that?!" Morgan said hoarsely.

Cassius could only stare in wonderment, stunned by what he could see and sense.

Eden floated inside a radiant sphere fluttering with red threads of bloodcursed magic, her clothes dancing against her body and her hair undulating in languorous waves around her face. Her pupils glowed scarlet and the devilwood staff blazed in her hand where she held it aloft, the runes covering its surface a brilliant blood-red.

Power poured into her and the weapon from a swirling mass of dark, lightning-charged clouds above them, bringing with it the acrid smell of sulfur and ozone.

Morgan scowled, his knuckles blanching on his swords. "That's the smell of the Hells! We have to stop her!"

Cassius shook his head. *"It is...and it isn't. Get ready, Morgan."*

Morgan glanced at him, confused.

"Eden is creating a chance for us to destroy Lucille's soul core," Cassius said.

"That power is mine!" the bloodcursed mage roared, her voice echoing with her master's fury.

She charged toward Eden, crimson spheres forming in her hands.

The air throbbed around Eden. Magic arced from the devilwood staff and slammed into Lucille, immobilizing her. Eden moved and grasped the stunned mage by the throat.

"Now!" she yelled at Cassius and Morgan.

They were at her side in the blink of an eye.

Lucille screamed as Cassius's lightning blade and Morgan's sword of wind pierced her front and back in one fell swoop. Cassius gritted his teeth. He felt her core fracture and disintegrate, the pain he always felt upon destroying another living being's soul rippling through him.

"Is it done?" Eden panted, sweat beading her forehead from the effort of channeling the magic she wielded.

"I think so," Cassius said stiffly as Lucille sagged silently on his and Morgan's blades. *"She's dying."*

Relief washed over Eden and Morgan's faces.

"You fools."

They froze at the sibilant voice that fell from the dying mage's lips. Lucille raised her head.

Morgan cursed as blackness filled the whites of her eyes.

"Do you think it's that easy to defeat a God?" Lucille's master said with a savage smile.

"*No.*" Cassius scowled. "*But we can cast you to the Nine Hells.*" He looked past the mage. "*Now, Eden! Use the staff!*"

Eden didn't hesitate. She drove the devilwood staff into Lucille's body, a roar of pure power ripped from her throat. Lucille's master bellowed in rage as darkness exploded on the mage's chest. Flesh and bone caved, the woman's mortal remains disappearing into the black hole with a sickening sound. Her master's scream faded into nothingness, along with the reek of his magic.

The black hole continued to grow.

Dread twisted Cassius's belly.

Morgan glanced at him, sensing his fear across their bond. "Cassius?"

"I—I can't control it!" Eden gasped, features locked in a mask of pain and knuckles white where she held the devilwood staff. "It's too strong!"

Morgan clenched his fists, finally grasping what was happening. "Fight it, Eden!"

The young girl gritted her teeth and bit her lip. The void swelled despite her best efforts.

Cassius grasped the devilwood staff and tried to yank it from her grip, heedless of the magic scorching his flesh. "*Dammit!*"

The only way to stop Eden's powers from consuming her was to break her hold on the weapon. Morgan closed his hands on the staff, black wind swirling around his fingers, his expression mirroring the determination filling Cassius.

"*Eden!*" someone shouted in a voice full of panic.

Brianna appeared in the mouth of the jagged opening in the building, Adrianne and the others alongside her. They froze, eyes rounding at the sight of the expanding void. Fragments of broken mirrors whined through the air and vanished into the hole. The debris littering the inside of the building followed.

"Stay back!" Cassius's feet dragged across the ground as the void pulled him in. *"This is a one-way ticket to the Nine Hells!"*

Brianna stumbled over the debris to reach her daughter. "Eden!"

Malik grabbed her arm and held her back.

"Let me go!" she snarled at the sorcerer.

"Keep her away from here, Malik!" Eden barked. She looked at Cassius and Morgan, a bittersweet expression dawning on her face. "Go! The devilwood staff will protect me wherever I end up! I will find a way back, I swear!"

Cassius clenched his jaw. He could see the lie in her eyes.

Eden looked over at Brianna. "I love you, mom!"

"Eden!" Brianna screamed.

Dryad magic throbbed through the air, a sea of green.

Cedric marched past Brianna, his blackthorn and alderwood crown coming to life even as leaves and twigs sprouted from his flesh, his laurel staff glowing in his grasp.

"Your Highness!" Galliad yelled as he entered the building. "You don't know what this will do to you!"

Cedric ignored the Dryad mage's warning, grass

and shoots blooming under his steps, his eyes shining with power. He walked past Cassius and Morgan, clasped Eden's face in his hands, and kissed her.

Eden gasped, her pupils flaring. The devilwood staff groaned in her fingers.

Cassius inhaled sharply.

The weapon was trying to gain control over its mage's magic and stop the impending catastrophe.

Branches shot out from Cedric, the growths thickening and twining rapidly until they encased his and Eden's bodies inside the trunk of a laurel tree. The building quaked and the ground shook as Dryad and bloodcursed magic collided inside the glowing sapling, the pressure wave almost driving Cassius and Morgan to the ground.

The black hole wavered for breathless seconds. It started shrinking, slowly at first, then with a speed that drew gasps from everyone. It vanished with an anticlimactic 'pop'.

Silence fell inside the broken House of Mirrors.

It was shattered by the sound of slithering foliage. The laurel tree was growing smaller. The branches and leaves thinned out and retracted, revealing the madly kissing couple inside.

The devilwood pendant levitated forlornly next to Eden while she stood in Cedric's hold, her arms around his neck, not a spare inch of space between their bodies and their lips.

Cassius swallowed a smile of relief and amusement.

The weapon looked almost grouchy standing witness to its mistress's passionate embrace.

"Like a goddamn fairy tale," Adrianne muttered, approaching with the others.

"Did Eden just open a doorway to the Nine Hells?" Julia asked Zach sotto voce.

"I think so," the demon muttered.

"We deserve a break after this," Bailey stated adamantly. "Oh, hey Charlie. You okay?"

The enchanter climbed the debris toward them, the Altered Mind box under his arm and a scowl on his face. "I can't believe you guys left me on that Ferris wheel!"

"Oh." Zach offered him a guilty face. "I thought I'd forgotten something."

Galliad pinched the bridge of his nose. "His Majesty is going to skin me alive when I tell him what his son has done."

"What did he just do?" Morgan asked.

Galliad sighed heavily. "That ritual is one that binds the magic of two soul cores. It is what Dryads do when they get married."

"What?!" Brianna squealed.

Cedric and Eden finally stopped kissing, faces flushed and eyes bright with emotion. They smiled at one another, oblivious to the crowd watching them.

"I am not happy about this!" Brianna snapped to no one in particular.

Malik scowled at the Dryad prince. "Let's just shoot him."

CHAPTER FORTY-ONE

"Well, well, well," Suzie Myers drawled. "This sure is a turnup for the books."

She propped her chin on her hand and gazed at the figures crowding the large booth in the middle of *Occulta*. Even though it was a busy Saturday night and the place was packed wall to wall with people, the bar's clientele was giving the group a wide berth.

Morgan made a face and paid for the drinks he'd ordered.

"Let's hope it's not a regular thing. My bank balance won't survive the ordeal."

Suzie arched an eyebrow. "Your bank balance owns the building you live in and several others in the city."

Cassius inhaled sharply, his hands on one of the trays of cocktails and beers. "Wait. You're my landlord?!"

Suzie smiled mischievously. "Oh. You didn't know?"

"No, I did not." Cassius scowled and stormed off, glass clinking dangerously.

Morgan's gaze dropped to the angel's swinging hips. He sighed dreamily.

"He sure has a nice ass," Suzie observed.

Morgan narrowed his eyes at her. "I thought you and Zach were a thing."

Suzie grinned. "We are a thing." She patted him on the shoulder and headed off to take care of the next patron's order. "I still have eyes, Morgan, and so do the rest of the people in this city."

By the time he brought the second tray to their booth, Morgan was in a foul mood. He'd caught at least a dozen people eyeing up Cassius as if he were forbidden fruit.

How the hell did I not notice it before? He studied Cassius broodingly where he sat next to Zach. *Maybe it's because people are less scared of him now. Which is a good thing.*

Morgan swallowed an unhappy sigh.

Adrianne's gaze swung from Cassius to Morgan and back. "What's wrong with you two?"

"I just found out this asshole is my landlord," Cassius said icily.

"Cassius is too damn good looking," Morgan grumbled.

Everyone stared.

"Wait," Adrianne said leadenly. "You *own* that building?!"

"What the hell are you talking about?" Cassius snapped at Morgan.

Morgan ignored Adrianne and narrowed his eyes at

the Empyreal. "I've caught scores of people staring at your butt in as many seconds."

"The only one staring at my ass was you," Cassius said between gritted teeth. "And can we drop this subject? We have a minor at the table."

Eden sat with her soda halfway to her mouth, flushed and mouth agape as she stared at Cassius and Morgan.

"Oh," Morgan muttered. "Sorry, Eden."

"Sorry Eden my tushie," Cedric grumbled where he sat next to her. "Mind your language around my girlfriend."

Eden choked on the sip of soda she'd just taken.

Brianna patted her on the back and glared at Cedric.

"I have not approved your relationship yet, Dryad!" she hissed.

"Your Highness," Galliad chided her gently.

"Your Highness," Brianna growled.

Malik glowered at the Dryad prince from where he sat sandwiched between Charlie and Bailey.

"There's nothing to approve of." Cedric shrugged, his expression smug. "Eden is my wife."

"What?!" Eden gasped.

Morgan stared. "Wait. You didn't tell her what you did back at the amusement park?"

"I tried several times, but some people kept butting into our conversation." Cedric frowned pointedly at Brianna and Malik.

Galliad told Eden about the sacred ritual Cedric had performed to save her life.

"It does mean you're technically married," he said at the end.

Eden paled.

Galliad's face softened. "Dryads mate for life. It takes most of us several centuries to find someone whose soul core magic matches our own. That is the person we are destined to spend the rest of our life with. Once soul core magic touches like yours did, the bond formed is breakable only by death."

Cedric took Eden's hand, his expression serious. "It is rare for Dryads to meet life partners from other races. That's why I resisted this for so long. But I can no longer fight my fate." He pressed a kiss to her knuckles. "I have found the one I am meant to be with."

Color flooded Eden's face.

"How romantic," Zach said with a smile.

Julia grinned and sipped her cocktail. Brianna stared at Eden and Cedric's clasped hands as if they were a bomb.

"Dryads are long-lived," Cassius said quietly. "Your existence will surpass Eden's. Is that something you are willing to accept?"

Silence fell around the table.

Morgan masked a frown at what he sensed behind his lover's warning. He couldn't help but feel that the separation Cassius spoke of mirrored their own relationship.

Is he talking about our past?

"Now that Eden's bloodcursed magic is stable, she will live longer than most humans," Cedric said, undaunted. "Having a Dryad partner means her lifespan can be multiplied several times over, since I can share my soul core magic to extend her existence. Being of royal blood makes that doubly so. Eden will likely survive as long as I do."

"There is still the subject of your family, Your Highness," Galliad reminded the prince.

Cedric grimaced.

Brianna frowned. "What do you mean?"

"As Dryad royalty, Prince Cedric's marriage would likely have been arranged with a Dryad whose family his father would have wanted to form a political alliance with. Though His Majesty married for love, that is not always the case for the princes and princesses of the Dryad kingdom. They are expected to sacrifice their own happiness for the greater good of our people."

"I'm sure mother and my brothers will have a lot to say on this subject, as will father," Cedric acknowledged grudgingly. "But still, they cannot refuse my bride. She is the most powerful mage in all the realms and can summon magic from the Nine Hells."

Eden went beetroot red.

Morgan suspected this had more to do with the fact that she was Cedric's wife than with the reality of her newfound status.

"You realize my daughter is still in high school, right?" Brianna said frostily.

"Of course." Cedric dipped his chin. "I am willing to wait until she is eighteen for us to wed formally. We shall call it an engagement for now."

Eden choked on air.

"Twenty," Brianna snapped.

"Twenty-five," Malik growled. "And after she graduates from college."

Eden spluttered, eyes rounding like marbles.

"You better say something, kid, or else you'll be getting married at fifty!" Adrianne hissed at the young girl.

"Well, this is a surprise," someone said coolly.

They turned.

Jasper Cobb and Reuben Fletcher stood next to their booth.

"I heard you and Cassius got your asses handed to you by a mage and her sister," Jasper told Morgan, his tone snide.

"I see fake news spreads like wildfire," Morgan retorted nastily.

Reuben smiled. "So, it isn't true?"

Morgan narrowed his eyes.

The angel and the demon chatted briefly to Brianna and Galliad before heading for the bar.

"I still can't believe those two are a couple," Julia murmured.

Morgan studied the proprietary hand Reuben laid on Jasper's back.

I still can't believe the demon is the bottom.

"Reuben's a saint," he mumbled.

Cassius rolled his eyes.

Charlie excused himself and headed in the direction of the restroom.

Galliad watched his back thoughtfully as he disappeared in the crowd.

"Why has he not been promoted to a Level One enchanter yet? He is more than able to hold that title, especially after what he did at that amusement park."

"He claims it was the Altered Mind box that did all the work," Adrianne said with a sigh. "Which is a lot of cockwaffle. We all know he's a Level One and we've been pushing him to apply for the promotion exam for ages. He's the only one who won't accept his abilities."

It had been Cassius's suggestion that Charlie use the Altered Mind box to create a trap for *Ouroboros*. Though the enchanter had protested he would not be able to use the device, it hadn't taken him long to master it. A simple enchantment would not have worked to lure Lucille and Valerie into believing they'd gained the upper hand. Argonaut needed a largescale and realistic spell and the only thing that could create that was the device that had fallen into their hands and an enchanter strong enough to wield it.

"That's a shame," Galliad murmured. "He has a lot of potential."

Morgan frowned into his drink. He wondered if they would ever be able to convince Charlie of his own worth.

"Will you visit the Dryad kingdom?" Cedric asked Morgan.

Morgan blinked. "I'm…still thinking about it." He felt Cassius's stare. "What?"

"We haven't been able to find out anything about our past or the one who was manipulating Chester and Lucille from the shadows," Cassius said in a levelheaded voice, all traces of animosity gone. "We may very well find the answers we seek in the other realms, like Bostrof said. And the deities there may know something of the God behind all of this."

Unease swirled through Morgan.

It had been ten days since their showdown with *Ouroboros* and the Hartman sisters. Though Argonaut could not officially tell San Francisco PD the details of the incidents concerning the bloodcursed mage, Morgan suspected Lambert and Willis would eventually find them out through the grapevine.

Galliad and Cedric had approached him shortly after the battle ended. They'd told him of their suspicions when they'd first witnessed his Demigod powers in the underground magic market. That he had Dryad blood in him. Their intuitions had proven to be correct.

The new power Morgan had unleashed when he'd fought Lucille and the crown that had appeared on his head marked him as someone who could wield ancient Dryad magic.

Galliad had informed Morgan that he was likely a direct descendant of Atlanteia, the first Dryad Queen and Goddess. Only direct scions of the original Dryad kings and queens could manifest an oak crown.

Morgan still wasn't sure what to make of any of it. Strickland had told him to keep his new powers a secret for now. The supernatural agencies were already in an uproar about the fact that two Demigods had been walking the Earth for five hundred years and now worked for Argonaut. From the little Strickland had revealed, the matter was still being discussed at the highest levels of the four organizations.

It was a comfort to Morgan that he knew of at least two heads who would support them. Those of Argonaut and Cabalista.

Victor Sloan was unlikely to tolerate any further injustice toward Cassius.

Morgan hadn't told Strickland or Cassius that he'd recalled Cassius's true name for an instant in the midst of that battle, before the spell that had caused all the Fallen to forget their past had kicked back in and erased it from his consciousness.

Next time. I'll remember his name next time. And I will kill the bastard who wiped all our memories when I get my hands on him.

Warm fingers landed atop his clenched fist. Morgan looked up into Cassius's steady gaze.

"It's okay. We don't have to go if you don't want to."

Morgan swallowed and turned his hand over to clasp Cassius's. "I'll go."

Surprise widened Cassius's eyes. "Are you sure?"

Morgan kissed Cassius's hand and smiled. "I'm sure."

Adrianne's face brightened. "Do I hear the word 'holiday' coming up?"

"Humans are not allowed in our realm," Cedric said flatly.

Adrianne's face fell. "*What?!* That's blatant discrimination!"

"I'll send you a postcard," Julia told the sorceress.

Zach grinned.

Malik's cell rang. He checked the display and frowned.

"Excuse me, I have to take this."

He rose and made for the exit.

"By the way, mom," Eden murmured as the sorcerer navigated the crowd. "When are you going to ask Malik out on a date?"

Brianna spat out her beer.

Eden handed her a napkin.

"*What*—what do you mean?!" Brianna squeaked, dabbing at her mouth and the stain on her dress.

"Well, from what you told me, there's no chance you and dad are getting back together," Eden said with a shrug. "It's clear Malik has a thing for you. And I'm pretty sure you like him too."

"I do?" Brianna mumbled, color staining her cheekbones.

"The chemistry between you two is off the charts," Julia said with a nod.

"Yup. We're talking Fourth of July fireworks here, lady." Adrianne leaned across the booth and dropped her voice to a conspiratorial whisper. "I bet sex between you is so good you won't be able to walk the next day."

Eden bit her lip.

Brianna groaned and dropped her flaming face in her hands.

Malik reappeared.

"Why is everybody looking at me like that?" Concern replaced the sorcerer's confusion when he saw Brianna. "Is Brianna okay?"

Brianna groaned some more.

"Oh, she's more than okay," Adrianne said with a dirty smile. "Or she will be once you do the dance of the two-headed—"

Julia elbowed the sorceress violently in the ribs.

THE END

Cassius and Morgan's adventures continue in Edge Lines.

AFTERWORD

I hope you enjoyed Spellbound, the second book in Fallen Messengers. This is my first MM urban fantasy romance series and I'm having such a blast mixing all my favorite genres. I hope you liked Eden and Cedric's story as much as Cassius and Morgan's. I would love it if you could leave a review of Spellbound on Goodreads or on the store where you purchased it. Reviews help readers like you find my books and I truly appreciate your honest opinions about my stories.

Make sure to sign up to the store newsletter for special deals on my books and new release alerts.

Or you can sign up to my author newsletter instead to get upcoming release notifications, sneak peeks, and giveaways.

BOOKS BY AVA MARIE SALINGER

FALLEN MESSENGERS

Fractured Souls - 1

Spellbound - 2

Edge Lines - 3

Oathbreaker - 4

Harbinger - 5

Crimson Skies - 6

CONTEMPORARY ROMANCE WRITTEN

AS A.M. SALINGER

Nights Series

Twilight Falls Series

ABOUT THE AUTHOR

Ava Marie Salinger is the pen name of an Amazon bestselling urban fantasy author who has always wanted to write MM urban fantasy romance. When she's not dreaming up hotties to write about, you'll find Ava creating kickass music playlists to write to, spying on the wildlife in her garden, drooling over gadgets, and eating Chinese food. She also writes contemporary MM romance as A.M. Salinger.

Visit Shop AD Starrling and buy all of Ava's ebooks, paperbacks, hardbacks, and exclusive special edition print books direct.

www.ingramcontent.com/pod-product-compliance
Lightning Source LLC
Chambersburg PA
CBHW060800190726
48285CB00002B/500